Lethal Allure

LETHAL ALLURE

The Cowboy Justice Association:
Serials and Stalkers
Book Two

By Olivia Jaymes

www.OliviaJaymes.com

CHAPTER ONE

LUKE "BREW" BREWSTER had grown up in a house full of women. His mother, of course, and his four sisters. Even the dog had been a female, so Luke and his father had been outnumbered at all times. It hadn't been easy either. With four sisters, he hadn't had much time in the bathroom and at one point in his childhood he'd been surrounded by literally dozens of stuffed animals, an unknown number of naked Barbies, and various shades of the color pink.

Mostly, he and his dad would hide out in the garage, watching sports and messing with an old car they were fixing up. Eventually, Brew's mom would shoo them back into the house for dinner and they'd all sit down together to talk about anything and everything. Frankly, he'd had an amazing childhood and was quite close to his family. Even with work, he tried to hang out with them at least once a week if possible.

So Luke thought he had at least a working understanding of the female mind. He knew about cramps, and mood swings. He understood that his sisters might talk about their problems but that didn't mean they wanted him to fix things for them. He didn't really understand why they were attracted to certain guys but he sure as shit understood that many of them were losers and didn't deserve any woman based on how they'd treated his sisters.

But he'd realized today that there was a gap in his education regarding women…

What in the hell was a *window treatment*? And how was it different than curtains? He'd agreed to help his little sister Melissa hang her window treatments this morning as she'd recently moved into a new condo.

He placed his toolbox on the floor. "So, we're hanging curtains today?"

"We're hanging window treatments."

His gaze ran over the curtains draped over the back of a chair. "They look like curtains to me."

She pointed to the dark blue fabric on the chair. "Those are curtains, but we're also going to have a valance. I guess, technically, it's a cornice."

If a valance or a cornice smacked him upside the head he wouldn't know the difference.

"Whatever you say. I'm just the muscle so tell me what to do."

Groaning, Melissa rolled her eyes. "You're such a Neanderthal sometimes, big brother. It wouldn't kill you to learn a little about interior design."

"You don't know that for sure. It might kill me."

"Tougher things have tried and you're still standing."

True, I've been shot at more than the average person.

Melissa directed him to her bedroom where the cornice was being stored. It was basically a box covered in fabric that coordinated with the drapes. It covered the curtain rod and hooks because apparently having them show was a big decorating faux pas.

Who knew?

The only reason Luke had curtains in his house at all was because his sisters had hung them. They'd also bought him throw pillows and various bric a brac that they claimed made a house homier. He'd always tease them and say that the pillows just matched his giant flat screen television.

The work didn't take long, however, and within an hour the drapes and cornice were hung over the front window. Luke had to admit that it did look nice.

"What's next?" he asked, popping open the beer that his sister had handed him after a job well done. "A new garbage disposal? Maybe a back deck?"

"You can't build a new deck," she scoffed, flipping on the television. "You're handy but that would take real skill."

"I think Dad and I could handle it. I'm actually pretty impressed that you built that cornice thing all by yourself. You needed tools for that. Did you buy yourself a hammer and a screwdriver?"

He'd thought about getting her a small standard toolkit as a housewarming gift, but he hadn't wanted to discourage her from asking him for help when she needed it.

Melissa laughed. "Are you kidding? I had my friend Shaw help me. There's no way I could do that by myself."

"Shaw? Is that some new guy you're seeing?"

"Shaw is a girl. She just has one of those names that is sort of neutral. I met her in yoga class about a year ago. She's really nice. And pretty."

Luke knew where this was going. His entire family seemed to think his single status was an affront to mankind. In truth, at age thirty-three he was getting a little tired of dating, but his job wasn't conducive to meeting women, nor were the hours. He worked a great deal and he hadn't yet met a female he liked enough to make compromises for. He definitely wanted to settle down some day, though.

"If you're to be believed, all your friends are pretty."

"Naturally. But I'm serious here. You and Shaw would make a nice couple." She hopped up from the sofa and grabbed her phone from the table. "Let me show you a picture of her. We all went out to the movies a few weeks ago."

"I'm not inter—"

"It won't hurt to look at her picture," Melissa scolded. "You might think she's attractive. Most people do."

His sister paged through her photos and then turned the screen so he could see. It was a picture of Melissa sitting in a movie theater with a friend on either side. He knew the one on the left was Taylor. He'd met her at his sister's birthday party last year. The other woman was a delicate little blonde with a big smile.

She was attractive. Really attractive. Luke might not admit it out loud, but he had a thing for blondes. Even better if they were petite. He was a big man, but he liked a woman he could perch on his knee and cuddle.

Melissa pointed to her friend. "That's Shaw. Isn't she pretty?"

"She is."

"She's nice too. And smart. And successful. She has her own business."

She sounded like a real paragon of virtue.

"Then she probably has more men than she knows what to do with."

"She's more of an introvert and she's not seeing anyone right now. I could fix you up."

Luke couldn't think of anything more terrible than being fixed up on a blind date by his little sister. He could get a date. If he wanted to. He'd just been damn busy lately with his new job.

"If she's so great, why is she single?"

"Why are *you* single?" Melissa shot back. "Because you work all the time and you're picky, that's why. It's the same with Shaw. Maybe I shouldn't try and fix you up after all. Especially, if you're going to be a grouch about it. Geez, when was the last time you went out on a date, anyway?"

Two...no...more like four months ago. It had been a waitress from the sports bar he and his co-workers liked to frequent. It hadn't been bad, but he hadn't felt the spark. Now it was awkward when he'd go for a beer with the guys. He should have known better but she'd basically asked him out, bold as brass. He'd said yes and now he only had himself to blame.

"A while ago," he finally replied. It wasn't any of her business. "Listen, she sounds like a nice woman but I'm so tired from working I don't think it's fair to date right now. This is my one day off this week and look how I'm spending it…with my sister. Some females want to be the center of attention and I can't give them that."

Melissa made a face and her gaze dropped down to her phone. "Celia liked to be the center of attention."

She hadn't said the words loudly, but Luke heard her. Celia was his high school girlfriend. He'd dated her for four years and they'd certainly been serious. At one point, he'd thought he might marry her. They'd broken up in a mutual decision about six months after high school graduation.

"Celia was a nice girl."

Because she was. Or at least she had been.

"Whatever happened to her?"

"Last I heard she got married and had a couple of kids. Why?"

Melissa shrugged. "Just wondered. You aren't still in love with her, are you?"

"No, and might I remind you that you're the one that brought her up, not me. I haven't thought about Celia in a long time."

"Shaw wouldn't want to be the center of attention. She avoids the spotlight."

"Good for her."

"So?" Melissa challenged, elbowing Luke in his ribs. "Should I fix you two up? I'm totally serious. I think you two would really hit it off. She's one of my best friends and it would be nice if your girlfriend was someone that the whole family would like."

"No."

"One date. That's all. It wouldn't hurt."

"No."

"C'mon, she's really nice. One measly little date. Just coffee. If you don't like her, I'll never say anything about the women you date ever again."

Now that was a deal worth making. Shutting up Melissa forever sounded like nirvana.

"Promise?"

Melissa made an X over her chest with her finger. "Cross my heart and hope to die."

It was so tempting…

"I'll think about it."

"This is why you're single, big brother. All you do is think. You need to be a man of action."

Thankfully, his sister didn't know how much *action* he was or wasn't getting.

"I said I'll think about it. Don't push me."

"You're pathetic. All you do is work."

"My work is important. I catch the bad guys."

Really terrible, truly awful bad guys.

"I just don't want you to end up alone."

He didn't want that either, but sometimes he wondered if the right woman was even out there. She might not even exist.

And if she did, she might hate his job. That would be a deal breaker. No question.

CHAPTER TWO

TODAY WAS A day for Shaw to celebrate. She'd inked a deal to write an advice book. She was finally beginning to see the fruits of her hard work and it was exciting. Yes, there were parts of the job that were less than ideal, but for the most part she was living the dream.

Those *less than ideal* parts were also fairly recent. She was, however, determined to keep her head down and not lose focus on her goals. Everything else was simply a distraction which she didn't allow much of.

In fact, she took great pride in being a workaholic, which is why her friends had to pry her out of her house and drag her out to dinner to celebrate this momentous milestone with a fancy dinner at a snooty restaurant. She had to admit that she was glad they did. It was one thing to be an introvert, but it was something quite different to be a hermit. Lately, she'd been working so much she might qualify for the latter.

Her friend Melissa had ordered them a round of drinks and was now raising her martini glass. "Congratulations, Shaw. There's no stopping you now."

They clinked glasses and Shaw took a sip of her cosmopolitan, the cool, tart liquid sliding down her throat. It was delicious, and she enjoyed how the vodka warmed when it reached her belly. She needed to pace herself, however. She was a complete lightweight when it came to booze and they'd only just ordered their entrees. She didn't want to be a tipsy mess before she even had a chance to eat her expensive dinner.

"So what did you do today to celebrate?" Taylor asked.

Shaw had met Melissa at a yoga class about a year ago, and then she'd met Melissa's friend Taylor. They had all luckily hit it off and enjoyed spending time together. They all had a quirky sense of humor that other people sometimes didn't quite get. Shaw had often been called weird and strange when she was in high school. It had bothered her when she was young but as she'd grown older, she'd realized those words were more of a badge of honor. She didn't want to be just like everyone else.

"I worked. Just like every other day, I guess."

She had an online channel where she gave relationship advice to people who contacted her with their problems. It had started out small, just a project when she was working on her masters' degree. It had actually been a friend's idea – more of a dare, really – but now it was a full-time job that paid all of her bills. It had taken a great deal of work and sweat but she was reaping the rewards now.

Melissa took a sip of her martini. "Anything interesting in this episode? Hoarder behavior? Cheating? In-law problems? He's a dog person and she's a cat person?"

"I like to fool myself into thinking that all my shows are interesting," Shaw replied tartly, but with a wry grin. "But since you asked, this one is all about expectations. For example, if I was dating someone what are reasonable expectations to have for my birthday? Or Christmas? Or even just getting taken to the airport? I get so many questions about that, by the way. People want to be taken to the airport or picked up, but no one wants to do the actual picking up or dropping off. It's a relationship minefield."

"It's like no one has ever heard of a cab or a ride share," Taylor lamented. "I dated a guy that wanted me to take him to the airport at one in the morning on a weekday. *One in the morning.* We'd been dating for like…a month."

Shaw nodded in understanding. "Expectations. We all have them, but we rarely discuss them out loud. Then we get upset when our partner doesn't meet them. That's how passive aggressive behavior starts."

"I didn't get all passive aggressive," Taylor replied with a laugh. "I just got gone. Toodles. Life is too short. But that wasn't the only reason. He had issues. Lots of 'em. I didn't want his issues to become mine."

Melissa's brows rose. "Speaking of issues… Are you still getting messages from that creepy fan?"

As a person in the public eye, Shaw received more than her fair share of creepy, weird messages. Some, however, were more disturbing than others. Most of the time she shrugged off the angry, disgruntled subscribers and simply blocked them from her social media. This one was proving difficult, though. He'd been blocked several times but kept coming back under different personas. He'd been ratcheting up the drama as well, sending more frequent and bizarre messages, swearing undying devotion and sounding angry in the same sentence.

Her agent had told her to block and ignore. There were strange people all over the world and the vast majority of them were harmless, simply reaching out for contact with someone they thought might understand them. As someone who had studied psychology, Shaw agreed with that assessment, but the problem was knowing whether this person was in the normal ninety-eight percent or that dreaded two.

"He sends me a message or email just about every day," Shaw replied with a sigh. "It's gone from one or two a week to multiples every single day."

"What does he say?" Taylor asked with a visible shudder. "He doesn't ask for your underwear, does he?"

Shit, that hadn't even occurred to Shaw. Ick.

"No," she said firmly, shaking her head. "He does not. He talks about how I'm the only one that understands him and that I need to help him."

"He might be beyond help," Melissa muttered under her breath. "But knowing you, you tried to."

"I did but he didn't want to see a therapist or talk to anyone but me. He became angry that I wasn't helping, and he called me lots of names. That's when I blocked him."

"Good for you," cheered Taylor. "That will teach him."

Sadly, it wasn't that easy.

"Didn't work. He just kept creating more profiles. The minute I block one he gets another. It's like playing a game of whack-a-mole."

"He has a lot of time on his hands," Melissa said. "You have to give him credit for his persistence. Imagine what he could do if he put that much effort into a career or a real relationship. Have you talked to the police?"

"What? No." Shaw shook her head. "I don't think this warrants calling law enforcement. My agent says that this is normal when you have a job that's public facing. There are always going to be a few cranks, trolls, and creeps. I'm not worried about it."

"You should talk to my brother Luke. He used to be a cop and now he deals exclusively with serial killers and stalkers. He could tell you what to do," Melissa said, not letting the subject go. "I could call him for you."

"There's no need," Shaw assured her friend. "This isn't a big deal. It's just some messages and emails. He's a pain but I doubt he's dangerous or anything."

Melissa tapped the edge of her glass. "He probably is but I just can't forget some of the stories I've heard from my brother. It's better to be safe than sorry. Just let him read the emails. Let him – a professional – tell you that you have nothing to worry about."

Shaw frowned. "You think I need to be worried." She looked at Taylor. "What about you?"

Taylor shook her head. "I don't know. If you say you're not

worried, then I'm sure it's nothing. But I haven't heard these stories that Melissa is talking about. If I had I might vote differently."

Shaw was definitely the type to overanalyze a situation, thinking about it every which way until it was worn out and dead. Or moot. She'd made an effort not to do that with any of these "out there" fans that she'd acquired.

"It's all perfectly normal," she said again, parroting her agent's words. "Every person in the spotlight has followers that are strange. You block, ignore, don't engage, and move on with your life. So far it's worked."

"But he keeps on making new profiles," Melissa pointed out.

"But eventually he'll get bored. He'll start following someone else and he'll forget all about me, especially if I don't give him the attention that he wants. He'll move on to someone who will."

The waitress brought their entrees and the conversation veered away to more neutral topics. The weather, Shaw's upcoming travels, and Taylor's new boyfriend.

"Speaking of boyfriends," Melissa said. "Did I mention that my brother isn't seeing anyone right now?"

Holy hell. A fix up?

"Are you trying to fix me up with your brother? This has come out of nowhere. And no, I'm not going to talk to him about the messages I've been getting. It's no big deal."

"I believe you. You've convinced me. This is me trying to make a match. Luke's a great guy and you're a great person, too."

Melissa clearly adored her older brother. She sung his praises constantly. But that didn't mean that he would be a good boyfriend. Brother and boyfriend weren't the same thing.

"He is handsome," Taylor giggling, her cheeks pink. "And sexy. He's never shown any interest in me but if he did…I'd be all over that."

Melissa was giggling as well. "My brother is good-looking, and he's a great guy. He was over the other day helping me hang the window treatments we did, and it occurred to me that you two would be great together."

Really?

"How would we be good together?" Shaw challenged. Her love life had been anemic lately, but she wasn't ready to be fixed up on a blind date. Was she? "Do we have anything in common? Anything at all?"

"You're both workaholics," Melissa answered promptly, a grin on her face. "You both like comfort food and hanging out at home. Luke isn't a partier in the least. Maybe a few beers with his friends once in awhile but mostly he's a homebody. Like you."

But Melissa wasn't done. "He's smart, and funny, and successful. He works on that special task force that deals with serious crimes, and he gets paid pretty well to do it. Why wouldn't you go out with him? He's the whole package. I told him about you, and he thinks you're pretty."

Now Shaw wanted to hide her head underneath the heavy linen tablecloth. Jeez, Melissa had been talking about her?

Cringeworthy.

He probably thinks I'm a big loser who can't find a date.

Melissa passed her phone to Shaw. "That's a picture of him. He's handsome, isn't he?"

Shaw had to admit that the man in the photo wasn't ugly at all. Dark-haired and muscular, he had a nice smile with a dimple in one of his cheeks. He definitely resembled his sister, especially around the chin.

"He looks like you." Shaw handed the phone back. "But I'm not hard up for a man."

Melissa just smiled and tucked her phone back in her purse. "I know you're not, but when was the last time you actually went on a date? And just so you know, I asked Luke that question, too."

Shaw had to really think back. It had been awhile. But certainly not that long...?

"A few months ago."

Laughing, Melissa rolled her eyes. "That's exactly what he said, but then he couldn't recall anything about her or what they did, so I think it's been longer. Let me ask you a question. What was his name?"

"Eric," Shaw answered promptly. She distinctly remembered him because he'd played saxophone in a jazz band as a hobby. He'd also had issues just like Taylor's ex. One of them was that he couldn't seem to take no for an answer. She still heard from him from time to time, but she never replied.

Taylor and Melissa exchanged a glance.

"That was over five months ago," Taylor announced. "We remember him. You went to that music festival in May. He was clingy and whiny."

Had it been that long? It couldn't be. Or maybe it could. Time had flown because she'd been so busy.

And Eric was indeed clingy and whiny.

Melissa placed her fork on the edge of her plate. "Five months, Shaw. That's a long time between dates."

"It's not that bad. I've been working."

It sounded lame even to her own ears.

"One date. Just one. Have coffee with Luke. You don't even have to go to dinner if you don't want to. Just meet him. I think you'll hit it off. And if you don't, I'll never say another word about your love life."

"Ever?"

"Not one word," Melissa vowed. "I promised Luke the same thing."

Shaw's friend wasn't a busybody. She was sort of the...*cruise director* of their group. She liked to organize things and make sure everyone was happy and having a good time. Normally, Shaw was content to go with the flow because Melissa did a good job.

Taylor tapped the edge of her martini glass. "It's been months, girl. It's long past time to get back on the horse. Hell, the horse has probably done run away from the barn. Luke's a nice man. Even if you don't feel any sparks, you'll probably have a pleasant evening."

"Five months is not that long."

"It is." Melissa held up one finger. "A single date. What could it hurt? Worst case scenario you have a moderately nice time. Best case? You and I are in-laws for life."

That bold statement had all three of them laughing. The odds weren't in favor of Shaw and Melissa's brother falling madly in love and getting married.

"I'm not looking to get married or even get serious with anyone. I'm focused on my career."

"Luke is too," Melissa said. "That's why you'd be perfect for each other. It's a no pressure situation. He's not looking for a wife and you're not looking for a husband."

They weren't going to give up until Shaw gave in. It would be easier to simply say yes and let the chips fall where they may. The chances were high that she and Luke Brewster had fuck all in common.

"Fine. I'll meet him for coffee or lunch. No dinner or movie."

An hour or two out of her day and then she could go home and get back to work. To be honest, Shaw simply wasn't looking to become involved. With anyone. The timing was all wrong.

★ ★ ★

LATER THAT EVENING, Shaw and her friends finished their celebratory dinner and went their separate ways. Taylor was meeting up for a late drink with her new boyfriend and Melissa needed to get a head start on grading homework. She was a math teacher at a local middle school.

Shaw had left a lamp on in the living room so it wasn't completely dark when she arrived home. Normally, living alone and the dark didn't bother her in the least but after tonight's discussion with her friends she was a little bit more on edge than usual. Melissa hadn't specifically told them the stories she'd heard from her brother, but she really didn't have to. Shaw read the papers and watched the news. She'd also studied criminal psychology so she was well aware of what one human being could inflict upon another. Often without any remorse whatsoever.

Consequently, she flipped on far more lights than usual, even the bright fluorescents in the kitchen for a few minutes until it was time to go to bed. The house was lit up like an airport runway but it made her feel better. She also turned on the television in her bedroom because then it sounded like there were friendly people in her home.

I've really lost it. I'm such a wuss.

She changed into her pajamas, took off her makeup, brushed her teeth, and settled into bed with her book. A lighthearted whodunit set in Paris. She'd never been there but it was on her bucket list. She couldn't seem to get past the first two paragraphs, however. That little voice in her ear wasn't going to leave her alone. Eventually she gave up and reached for her laptop sitting on the bedside table.

She opened her email and there was another message from Eric. She'd blocked his texts quite a while ago, but she hadn't bothered with his email address. She probably should, though. This letter wasn't anything exciting. He wasn't pushy or threatening. He kept saying that he still wanted to be friends. To that end, he'd send her emails about once a week telling her about what he was up to and the things he was planning. Then there was the usual invitation for her to contact him if she wanted to join in. Which she didn't. But he wasn't being an asshole, he was just being oblivious. He was completely harmless, of that she was sure. Closing her email and opening up her channel's account, she checked her messages, quickly scanning through them.

There it was. Another one from *him*. Well...she assumed it was a him. He talked like he was a guy, although no one on the internet would know if it was a tabby cat sending her disturbing messages.

It was another new profile, but she only had to read through the subject and then the contents to know it was the same person. He always signed off the same way...

I love you, Shaw. More than you can possibly know.

That was a kind of love that she didn't want or need.

Her agent had assured her that these people just wanted attention. It was a fact that she knew well from her own studies. When he didn't get it, he would move on to someone else. But he'd been persistent as hell. She hadn't expected him to be this dogged in his pursuit of her attention.

At first, she'd tried responding to him. The first few messages hadn't been all that creepy. He'd told her how pretty she was and how much he enjoyed her channel. She'd sent a message back thanking him which is what she did with all her messages unless they were downright nasty. Apparently, he'd taken her reply as the signal that she wanted a far more personal relationship with him than content provider and channel subscriber. After that a barrage of messages and emails had come in until she'd finally blocked him. Then, he'd simply created a new persona.

This had been going on for almost two months, and he was clearly not happy about being blocked over and over. At first, he'd said he was disappointed in her reaction. Then as it had continued, he'd said she was *making him angry* and she needed to stop. Which of course begged the question…

Or he'll do what?

He'd simply sent more messages. So she blocked him again tonight. But first, she saved the message off into a folder. Each week she'd show her agent so she could reassure Shaw that it wasn't unusual or strange. That it was no big deal.

This is life in the public eye. I better toughen up and get used to it.

After hitting the button, Shaw crossed her fingers and hoped that *this* time would be the last.

SETTLING INTO HIS *chair, he opened his laptop and checked his messages. She'd ignored him. Again. Blocked him. Again. He was tired of her behavior. She acted as if he didn't exist. Like he was*

nothing. She didn't understand about fate and destiny. She didn't understand at all. But he'd make her see. Eventually, she'd be all his.

Opening one of his desk drawers, he pulled out her blue scarf and wrapped it around his palm. Soft and silky, just like her hair. He pressed it to his face and rubbed the fabric against his skin. Her scent filled his nostrils, light and floral, and his body tightened in response. His sweet Shaw.

With his left hand, he unbuttoned his pants and slid the zipper down...

CHAPTER THREE

S HAW COULDN'T FIND her blue scarf with the white flowers. It had to be somewhere because scarfs couldn't grow legs and walk away, at least not in real life, but she'd ripped her bedroom apart and it was nowhere to be found.

Wracking her brain as to when she'd worn it last, all she could remember was that it was a movie night with her friends. She was positive that she'd taken it off and tucked it in the bottom drawer of her dresser, but it wasn't there.

So she'd checked every drawer. Then her closet. Then the linen closet. After that, she'd been at her wit's end and had checked the room she used as her studio, and then the closet in her office. She'd even checked the pantry in her kitchen. The scarf was nowhere to be found.

She was beginning to think that she was losing her mind. To say the least, she had a great deal going on in her life and keeping organized was becoming a huge challenge. She'd never been one to make lists, but she was feeling more and more like she needed to do just that. With all that she had to do, she was becoming increasingly scatterbrained, misplacing items and forgetting to return calls.

Back in high school she'd done the same thing her sopho-
more year, but she'd buckled down and made an effort to keep
her homework papers and notes organized. She'd used a color-
coding system and it had certainly helped. It wouldn't help find
her scarf but clearly, she needed to slow down and pay attention
to what she was doing. Last week she'd misplaced her favorite
pair of sunglasses, a funky blue and pink pair she'd picked up in
the Caribbean while on vacation with some college friends. Now
it was a scarf. She was lucky her head was attached so she
couldn't lose it.

Finally giving up, she grabbed an ivory scarf on the way out,
locking the door behind her. The conversation with Melissa and
Taylor from the other night was still ringing in her ears and
she'd made sure to lock her deadbolt and leave a few lamps on
inside her home. She didn't like being paranoid, but they had
got to her a little. She was a sort of public figure and it wouldn't
hurt to be more careful, in general.

"Hey, Shaw. Great weather, huh?"

Her neighbor across the street, James Hornsby. A nice guy, a
bit of a loner. He was about her age, maybe a few years older,
and very friendly, always waving and chatting when she was
outside.

He did keep to himself, though. She'd never seen him have
many visitors. He traveled quite a bit though, so she assumed
that's when he did the bulk of his socializing. Today he was
dressed in blue sweatpants and a long-sleeved t-shirt. He must be

out for a run.

"Hi, James. It is a lovely day, although a bit chilly. I didn't realize you were back from your trip."

"Yesterday. I hiked part of the Appalachian Trail with a few friends. You should definitely do that."

Shaw couldn't think of anything she wanted to do less. She wasn't someone who wanted to carry a heavy backpack and then camp outside. She liked indoor plumbing and a firm mattress.

"I'll keep that in mind. It sounds like you had a good time."

"I did, but glad to get home." His gaze took in her attire and the keys in her hand. "Are you heading out?"

"I'm meeting someone for coffee."

He hesitated, opened his mouth to say something, and then snapped it shut abruptly.

"Then I won't keep you. Have a good afternoon. Stop by anytime if you like. I can show you pictures of my trip."

She wasn't ever going to do that.

"Thanks, I do really need to get on the road."

She didn't want to be late for her coffee date with Melissa's brother Luke. She had a pet peeve about punctuality even if she wasn't at all sure this entire situation was a good idea. She'd almost talked herself out of meeting him about a dozen times in the last two days.

Now the time had come. She was going to meet him and let the chips fall where they may. Would it be a dream date or a bust?

★ ★ ★

IT WAS ONLY a coffee date. No big deal. No huge commitment.

At least that was what Luke was telling himself as he walked down the sidewalk toward the coffee shop where he was meeting Melissa's friend Shaw Parker. His sister had convinced him – somehow – that doing this was a good idea. He was still skeptical. He was so focused on his career at the moment that he wasn't sure this was a good time to get involved with a woman. Melissa had told him that Shaw felt exactly the same, so he was doubly confused as to why they were meeting but his sibling simply wasn't going to give up until he said yes.

So he'd given in. Now here he was on the first blind date he'd been on in years. Wasn't that sort of pathetic? It wasn't that he couldn't find a good woman, it was that he didn't have time.

Or was it? Frankly, he'd been looking for a good woman for a long time and he hadn't found her. Not even close. He'd had a few decent relationships here and there that had lasted awhile, but he couldn't honestly say that he'd met anyone that he'd thought about settling down with. If he couldn't find a compatible female though, what chance did his sister have?

This is probably going to be bad.

To make matters even more humiliating, Melissa had told him that this woman had specified coffee or lunch. No dinner. No movie. Shit, he wasn't even worth a full evening. It did, however, make it easier to bug out if things became truly and terribly awkward. Normally, he'd use his work as a reason to end the date early, and his buddy Ryan was standing by ready to check in about forty-five minutes into the date. If it was going bad, Luke would make his apologies, pick up the check, and get out of there.

Entering the coffee shop, he paused near the doorway, his gaze scanning the room. There she was, at a booth near the back. Unlike most people, she wasn't hunched over her phone, tapping away at a text. Instead, she was reading a book. Nice. He had a pet peeve about humans being so obsessed with their phones. Hell, half the time they'd walk right into traffic without even looking up. Someone was going to get hurt or killed.

The shop smelled delicious, a mix of coffee, cinnamon, and chocolate. He'd become a regular patron of this place since it opened about a year ago. The service was fast and friendly, and the pastries were all homemade.

"Shaw Parker?"

Her head came up and she blinked at him a few times as if she'd been lost in her book. But she quickly set it aside, sliding a bright red bookmark in it to mark her spot for later.

"I'm Shaw. You're Luke Brewster?"

He was sure that she'd seen a photo of himself just as he had of her, but pictures could be deceiving. Luke liked to think that he looked better in person than in some ill-lit selfie on his sister's cell phone.

"I am." He slid in the booth across from her. "It's nice to meet you, Shaw. I hope I'm not late."

"It's nice to meet you, too. And no, you're not late." She

checked her watch. "In fact, you're one minute early."

"In a big family, if you're late you might miss out on seconds," Luke replied, trying to make a small joke to ease the tension of a blind date. "I learned to be punctual or starve."

Shaw slid the book onto the seat next to her, her hands fluttering nervously. "I...um...I'm an only child."

"Then you probably didn't have to arm wrestle for the last drumstick."

She didn't have a chance to reply because the waitress arrived at the table, pad and pencil in hand, ready to take their order. Shaw ordered a chai latte. Luke ordered a shot in the dark. He also talked her into sharing a slice of lemon cake with him. He could have easily eaten one – or more – himself but he didn't want her to think he was a glutton on the first date.

"What's a shot in the dark?" she asked when the waitress headed behind the counter to start on their order. "I've never heard of it before."

"Coffee with a double shot of espresso."

Her eyes widened. "That sounds...caffeinated."

"It is. Very. I discovered them when I was in college and I needed to stay up all night studying."

"And now?"

"Now I just like them when I haven't had much sleep. I've been burning the midnight oil lately on a case."

"You're a cop? I mean...sort of. Melissa said that you used to be but now you're on some sort of special task force."

Luke was always having to explain about his job. He didn't

mind it though because he loved what he did.

"I was a cop, but now I work for a private firm. They specialize in helping small towns and counties with complex cases that they might otherwise not have the manpower or experience to deal with. They don't want to have to hire a person that wants vacation and health insurance to deal with a murder that may only happen once every five years. Plus, they simply may not have the experience in dealing with cases like that. That's where we come in."

Shaw's delicate fingers played with the paper napkin. The nails were short but well-kept, painted a pale blue that just matched her eyes. She really was a beautiful woman with her pale blonde hair and porcelain skin. She was dressed casually in faded blue jeans and a red cotton sweater. The fall weather had turned quite cool recently.

"She said you specialized in serial killers and stalkers. That must be very interesting."

It was and if he wasn't careful, he'd talk about his work until her ears fell off. His sister had warned him when she'd set up this date. No talking about grisly murders. Melissa wasn't sure that Shaw would appreciate his enthusiasm for the puzzle of catching a killer.

"It is," he agreed, careful not to appear to be too eager to discuss dismembered bodies. "I'm lucky to be given a chance like this so young. I haven't been doing it long, but the cases are interesting."

The waitress returned with their drinks and food. Luke

poured a little sugar into his coffee and then took a sip. So good. This was definitely going to help him wake up. He'd been looking through missing person reports with Ryan until about two in the morning.

"So you have an online channel?"

Luke didn't want to hog the conversation. He wanted to know more about her. Melissa had made her sound amazing and so far, she seemed to be what his sister had promised.

But it was early yet.

Shaw took a small bite of the cake and nodded. "I do. It started out as sort of a lark while I was working on my masters' degree in psychology, but it's really grown and now it's my full-time job."

He'd heard quite a bit about her career, actually and he was impressed. It wasn't something he could do but he admired that she could get in front of the camera and put herself out there.

The fact was…Melissa had told him about Shaw's persistent "fan" that wouldn't take no for an answer. She'd asked his opinion, but he couldn't really give it as he didn't know the details or had read the messages.

Should I bring it up? Will I ruin a perfectly nice afternoon? Probably.

"So you give people relationship advice? Do they write in? How do you choose what to put on your channel?"

He decided to go with more general questions to keep the peaceful atmosphere.

Shaw's expression instantly brightened up at being asked

about her work, which Luke liked. He wanted to be with someone that was as passionate about their work as he was.

"They do write in and I look for themes in the problems. For instance, I just did a show about boundaries in relationships. Not just romantic ones, but friends, family, and co-workers. We as humans are conditioned to give into people so that we're *nice.* Being a nice person is really valued but when that niceness comes at too high of a price and our boundaries get stomped on it's bad for the person. People need healthy boundaries with others."

"I can see what you're saying. I had a guy I used to work with that always tried to get everyone to pay for his beers or food when we went out after a long day. He always had a reason that he couldn't pay. Bills, a girlfriend, a sick dog. Whatever. Eventually, we all kind of got tired of covering him all the time and then he'd get pissed off and say we weren't being good bros."

"And then out of guilt, someone would give in," Shaw guessed with a nod. "That's common. People like that don't see boundaries the way you or I do. They only see obstacles to be overcome. The means or method doesn't matter. That person's feelings don't matter. Only the goal does."

"That's one of the signs of a sociopath."

"True, but just one. The latest research says that sociopaths make up about four percent of the population but remember that it's a spectrum. Not everyone is going to go out and commit crimes."

Chuckling, Luke took a sip of his coffee. "I wasn't saying

they would, just making an observation about boundaries. Sounds like an interesting show. I might have to check it out."

Shaw's cheeks turned pink. "Sorry, I get sort of passionate about my work. In fact, I have a meet and greet scheduled next week for some of my subscribers. I've done about a half dozen of these around the country. I rent out part of a restaurant, order a bunch of food and then talk to them, answering their questions. That sort of thing. My agent says that it's important to have create personal connections since my job is online and rather impersonal."

"I think that's a good thing. I'm that way about my work too. It's not just a job to me. It's far more."

She nodded in understanding. "I feel passionate about my work too. Helping people is important to me. I don't do it for the attention. In fact, I'd rather not have any of that."

It was an opening. Should he bring up her fan now?

He didn't get a chance too, however, as she continued speaking.

"So this is probably when I should say that my career is the number one thing in my life right now. I'm not sure why I agreed to this blind date as I work most of the time. I rarely go out and socialize. I feel like I have to strike while the iron is hot, if you know what I mean. The opportunities that I have now won't necessarily always be there and I don't want to waste them."

Ouch. He felt the same, but it was tough being on the other end of the speech.

He pointed his fork toward the half-eaten lemon cake. "How about we wait until after we finish this before we decide to get married and have kids?"

Her mouth fell open in shock at his outrageous statement but then her full pink lips widened into a grin and she began to laugh. Her blue eyes sparkled and her cheeks turned red, and he was once again reminded of just how attractive Shaw Parker was.

Slapping a hand over her mouth, she shook her head. "I'm so sorry. Again. I was so intent on getting that out there that I didn't think about how pushy and cold it sounded. I swear I'm not usually so ill-mannered and awkward."

Luke liked a woman that could laugh at herself. And at him. He also liked that she could apologize, even though he didn't think she'd done anything wrong. He'd been around too many people that could never admit to being less than perfect.

"You're just fine," he assured her. "I kind of wanted to say the same thing but didn't know how to phrase it. My career is important to me too and I tend to work a lot. Anyone that I have a relationship with will have to deal with that. My hours are actually much more regular than when I was a cop, but they still aren't nine-to-five."

Shaw's brows rose. "Where does that leave us?"

That was a good question. Luke was definitely physically attracted to this woman, and so far, she appeared to be easy to get along with. His gut was urging him to move forward, ask her out again and see where it all might lead.

"How about it leaves us cautious?" he replied. "We take

things slowly and don't look too far ahead. Just enjoy ourselves this afternoon, and then decide if we want to do it again. If we do, take it one date at a time. If either of us wants to stop, we do it. No hard feelings and stay friendly. After all, you're one of my sister's best friends."

"One date at a time," she repeated, nodding her head. She looked like she agreed. "So at the end of a date we decide if we want to repeat it? Interesting. I like not having to look too far in the future."

"We just keep things casual. I'm guessing we'll eventually figure out if we hate each other."

"Casual. That's a great way to describe it. We're casual with each other. I won't expect us to go out every Saturday night or stuff like that. If we keep the expectations low at the beginning, then that should also keep the stress low as well."

"And who doesn't want less stress?" Luke laughed. "It sounds like we have a plan."

"Plans are good. Now tell me more about your job. It sounds really interesting."

Luke hoped she meant that because he was going to do as she asked. By the end of this date, she might never want to see him again.

★   ★   ★

LUKE BREWSTER WAS a nice man. Funny, charming, and obviously intelligent. He was everything his sister had promised.

He was good looking too. Handsome and yes, sexy. Dark-haired with soft blue eyes, he was a big man, well over six feet tall with wide shoulders and muscular thighs that stretched his denim jeans. All the furniture around him seemed too small for his frame, as if he was normal-sized but the coffee shop was a dollhouse. Even his hands were big and she had no doubt that he could break her in half if he wanted to. She didn't feel threatened, however, as he seemed quite mild-mannered as they chattered away over coffee and cake.

Her phone buzzed on the table and she quickly checked it. Taylor. They'd made a deal to check in during the date in case she needed a quick exit strategy. Her friend had been adamant that Shaw wouldn't need it as Luke was a great guy, but she'd offered it anyway. Just in case they didn't hit it off.

His phone buzzed just seconds later as she was typing out a quick response.

It's going fine.

He was tapping out a reply too.

"Did you have a friend checking in?" he said with a grin. "Mine was making sure I didn't need a work emergency to get me out of here."

Shaw's mouth fell open. He'd had a backup also? She wasn't sure how to feel about that. She'd had one, of course, but it hadn't occurred to her that he might as well. But it really made sense. He'd probably been as nervous and wondering whether this was even going to work out.

"Taylor offered," she finally answered. "I thought it might be a good idea. You know, in case we didn't hit it off and ended up arguing about politics and which actor was the best Doctor Who."

"David Tennant," Luke replied immediately. "But I'll give Matt Smith honorable mention. I sure as hell don't want to talk about politics, though. That might be dangerous."

She wrinkled her nose. "Would it be awful if I said that I avoid the news these days? It's just all so depressing sometimes."

"I'm a news junkie but I promise not to tell you anything unless we're invaded by little green men from outer space."

"Deal, although I'd probably figure that one out on my own."

They continued chatting over the rest of the dessert. Shaw talked about several of the episodes she'd done for her channel, and he'd spoken about a few of the cases that he'd worked. As conversations often do, they'd come full circle back to her career. The cake was long gone and their cups were empty. It was getting close to the time to wrap up the date. Two and a half hours had flown by.

Rubbing his chin, Luke grimaced. "I wasn't going to mention this at all but since we're back talking about your career…"

Shaw had a feeling about what he was reluctant to bring up. If they were going to see each other again – and it looked like they would – they might as well get this over with.

"Go ahead," she urged. "I'm guessing Melissa told you about it."

"She did," he agreed. "She mentioned that you have a fan

that might just be far too enthusiastic. He won't go away."

"That's the long and short of it. I keep blocking him and he keeps creating new profiles. My agent says that this is par for the course with a public career and that I shouldn't give him any attention. Eventually he'll go away on his own and bother someone else who will give him that attention that he craves."

"Do you agree with that assessment?"

"For the most part I do. Most of these people that message me are annoying but they're not going to hurt me. They get off on being anonymous."

"Keyboard warriors?"

Shaw nodded. "Exactly. They'd never have the guts to say those things to me in person, but on the internet no one knows you're a cocker spaniel."

It was her go-to joke and he did laugh, thank goodness. He seemed to get her strange sense of humor, which was a relief. She'd been on a date a few years ago and the man had told her in no uncertain terms that she wasn't funny at all. She'd been home before nine that night. Looking back, he hadn't had much of a sense of humor. He hadn't cracked a smile the entire date. Not one.

"I'm not sure about the whole cocker spaniel thing. Do you know how hard it has to be to type with paws? It's most likely a raccoon. They have thumbs."

The thought of a raccoon sending her mean messages on the internet had her giggling.

"I'm picturing an angry raccoon pounding on his keyboard,

commenting on Facebook," she laughed. "Thank you for the image. This one's going to stick."

"It might be a monkey," he went on, a smirk on his handsome face. "But I doubt it's a penguin. Those wings would make it difficult to type as well. You can probably take a lion or tiger off the list too."

Shaw tried to keep a straight face. "I've heard bears are quite socially conscious, so it might be a grizzly."

"Or Bigfoot. He's just trying, in his own socially inept way, to reach out to society. He just wants to belong."

"I think I should say at this juncture in our relationship that I'm not sure that I believe in Bigfoot. The Loch Ness Monster? Sure, that's a no brainer. She's real. But Bigfoot? I'm a hell of a lot more skeptical."

Luke's lips twitched with laughter. "I think you're right to be. In this age of cell phones, shouldn't there be a photo of him by now? With all the lost phones, you'd think he'd find one, take a selfie, and get an Instagram account."

Still chuckling, Luke sat back in the booth. "I have a good friend who believes that Bigfoot is real. He actually makes a good case when you talk to him. I'd love it if he were right."

"You guys get along okay?"

"Sure, he respects that I'm the type that needs more evidence and I respect his belief that he has all the evidence that he needs." Luke leaned forward, his elbows resting on the table. "Don't think that I haven't noticed that you've directed the conversation away from your number one fan. If you don't want to talk about it, it's fine. I don't want to force things."

"It's not that I don't want to talk about it," Shaw explained. "It's just that I'm not sure what's to be gained from it. I'm trying not to give him any attention, and I don't want him to take over my life. Honestly, I'm hoping to just ignore him and eventually he'll go away."

"That could happen."

Luke didn't look convinced.

"But you think it's unlikely."

"I didn't say that. I don't even know what he's been saying or how many times he's tried to contact you. I'm just saying that it could all go away. Most of these issues do resolve themselves."

"Some don't."

"That's true. The problem is you don't know which situation you have."

Shaw had known this was where they were headed.

"You want to look at his messages."

She didn't phrase it as a question, because it wasn't one. It was written all over his face. He was concerned, which was nice since they'd only just met today.

"I do," he confirmed solemnly. "Just let me read through them. I assume you've saved them?"

"I did, because my agent told me to." Shaw picked up her phone but didn't unlock it. Should she send them to him? She didn't want to make more of this than it already was. "I have all of them in a folder. But…"

"You don't think it's all that bad?"

"I'm sure it's nothing. You'll be wasting your time, and I know you're busy with your new job because Melissa told me so. *You* told me so."

"They let me eat and sleep. You don't have to send them to me if you don't want to, but it might give you peace of mind to have someone else's opinion."

What if his opinion didn't agree with her own? Was she the type to stick her fingers in her ears and sing over anyone that disagreed? She'd always prided herself on being open-minded. Now it was time to put that to the test. If she believed that her fan wasn't any threat, what would be the harm in letting him look at the messages?

"I'll send them to you."

He was going to see that the entire situation wasn't anything to worry about. Everything was just fine.

CHAPTER FOUR

LATER THAT EVENING, Shaw took a long, hot bath, soaking as she replayed her date with Luke Brewster in her head. It had gone far better than she'd ever hoped. He'd been everything that Melissa – and Taylor – had promised. Handsome, funny, and intelligent. She'd found out that he also had a masters' in psychology, although he was clearly putting his degree to a different use. She was trying to help people and he was catching them when they were beyond that help.

A sense of humor was high on Shaw's list of attributes she needed a man to have and Luke had delivered on that and then some. That he was sexy, and his voice low and grumbly didn't hurt either.

He was also one of the largest men Shaw had ever met in her life. As in really, really big. That had only been highlighted when he'd walked her to her car, towering over her at least a foot and maybe more, his wide shoulders almost blocking out the sun. When they'd hugged goodbye though, he'd been extra gentle as if he was well aware of his own strength.

The hug had been lovely though, warm and comforting.

He'd smelled good too, a mixture of citrus and soap. Nice and clean without being overwhelming or heavy. Just…manly.

Okay, I'm a sucker for a nice-smelling guy.

It didn't hurt that he'd be the type to have her back in a dark alley. Not that she hung out in dark alleys, but he had an air about him that somehow said that he had it all under control and it was all going to be fine.

What kind of kisser would he be?

She'd found herself studying his lips at one point, wondering that very question. Far too early in the date to be thinking about it, but… She couldn't help herself. He was that attractive.

He'd definitely dated. They hadn't discussed their romantic histories yet but a man that good looking, sexy, and charming wasn't sitting home all by himself on Saturday nights watching television or playing video games. He was the kind of man that probably had women panting after him.

So why me?

If he'd wanted a girlfriend, he could go out and get one. Melissa said that he worked all the time, and Shaw could totally understand that. In theory, she wasn't ugly either and she'd had her share of male attention since hitting puberty, but she'd never considered herself a great beauty.

Did Luke Brewster find her as attractive as she found him?

Her phone ringing pulled her abruptly from her wandering thoughts. A quick check of the screen had her wincing in response.

Her mother. Julia Parker Stephenson, age fifty-five. She'd

remarried about six months ago to a man she'd met in San Francisco while on vacation with a friend. Shaw hadn't been too sure about the relationship, but they seemed quite happy.

Do I really want to talk to her right now?

If I don't answer, she'll just call again and again until I do. Might as well get this over with.

She dried her hand and pressed the speaker button.

"Hello, Mother."

"Shaw, I've been worried sick about you."

That tone. Shaw knew it well. That plaintive tone that said that she'd done something terribly wrong and hurt her mother. Again.

"Why? I'm fine."

"How would I know that? I haven't heard from you in over a week. You could have been dead in a ditch somewhere and I wouldn't have known."

Sighing internally, Shaw rolled her eyes. "I'm sure that if the police found me in a ditch, you'd be the first one they called."

"It's been over a week."

A blessedly peaceful one, too. It was almost as if Shaw's mother made everyone around her tense and on edge.

"I've been working, Mom, and you've been out of town. What can I do for you?"

Cut to the chase of the call. Bottom line it.

"Can't I call just to talk to you? Why does it have to be about anything in particular?"

Because there was always a reason. Shaw's mother didn't

chat.

"Of course, you can call me."

"I would hope so. I was in labor forty-eight hours with you."

And you'll never let me forget it.

"I didn't do it on purpose. Now how was your trip to Las Vegas? Did you and Oliver win any money? See any shows?"

They'd gone to celebrate the one-year anniversary of their first meeting.

"We didn't gamble all that much, at least I didn't. We played golf and saw the sights. You need to go see Hoover Dam. It's a feat of engineering."

"I'll put that on my list. What else did you do?"

"We ate at a few fancy restaurants, but I don't want to talk about that. It wasn't important. I want to talk about you. Did you hear from that publisher yet?"

It was strange that Julia didn't approve of Shaw's career but she sure as hell wanted to be involved in it. As deeply as possible.

"I did," Shaw replied reluctantly. This wasn't going to go over well. At all. "I signed the contract a few days ago."

She braced for the storm to come. Julia didn't like not being consulted about these things.

"What? You signed it already? What were you thinking, Shaw Catherine Parker? You can't just go around signing things. You need a lawyer to look over the contract."

So much for a relaxing hot bath.

"I did have an attorney look at it, Mom. We all agreed that it was a good offer."

"We? Who is we? I wasn't consulted."

Because I'm almost thirty years old. You don't control me any-more. You just think you should.

"Me, my agent, and the attorney. It's a good deal. You'll have to trust me on this."

Haha. Trust? That wasn't going to happen.

"You need to send me a copy of that contract immediately so I can look it over. I think you have three days to be able to get out of it."

"Mother, I don't want out of it."

Shaw tried to say it gently but she was losing patience. Her mother wasn't a lawyer or in publishing. She wouldn't know if it was a good or bad deal. She simply wanted to be in charge of it. She wanted to know all the details, especially when it came to her daughter's money. Julia had all sorts of ideas as to how Shaw should spend her newfound income.

"Send it to me right away. My God, you really need to be more careful. People can take advantage of you if you're not on guard."

Shaw had been talking to her friends about setting more boundaries with her mother. She didn't do well at that and it was something that she'd vowed she was going to do in the next year. She wasn't a child anymore, and she wouldn't give in to her mother's emotional blackmail. The whining, the crying, and the histrionics that frankly Julia should have grown out of by five years old. She'd do whatever it took to get Shaw to behave in whatever way she thought was right. Shaw's feelings?

Not all that important.

Sitting up in the tub, Shaw took a deep, fortifying breath. "Mother, the decision has been made. I signed the contract. It's a done deal."

There. Straight and to the point. No equivocation. Julia didn't get to meddle in her life anymore, pulling her strings.

Holy shit, I just shut down my mother.

Shaw's stomach twisted into a tight knot as she waited for her mother to explode. She'd probably see the fireworks in the sky from across town.

"I see," Julia said, slowly and deliberately. Shaw could practically see her mother seething through the phone. "I didn't realize that my opinion didn't count for anything anymore. I'm only your mother, the person who loves you and gave birth to you. Those agents and attorneys won't put you first like I will, but I can see that you've made up your mind."

There were a few sniffles to indicate that Julia was now crying. Shaw had made her mother cry. Oliver wasn't going to be happy, either. He hated it when his wife cried.

Shaw was literally shaking in the now cooling bathwater. This was when she normally folded like a cheap tent and gave in to whatever her mother wanted.

Not this time. I have to remind myself that she isn't going to add any value looking over that contract. She's not a lawyer.

"Mother, can we talk about something else? We aren't getting anywhere on this topic."

No justifying. Defending. Arguing. Just deflect. Redirect the conversation.

"Is there anything else you've done that I should know about? Perhaps you got married while I was away? Had a few children?"

Ah, sarcasm. The tears hadn't worked so Julia had found another arrow in her quiver.

"No, still single."

She didn't mention her date with Luke Brewster. Her mother always found fault with anyone she dated.

"If you called me every now and then I wouldn't be wondering what is going on in your life."

"I'll call more, Mom."

The tent was slowing folding.

"Of course, you will. You're such a good daughter. Call me tomorrow morning. Oliver and I are going to watch television now."

"Have a nice night."

Shaw disconnected the call.

What would I tell myself if I asked me for advice?

Don't be a pushover.

When it came to Julia Stephenson, that was easier said than done.

AFTER HIS MEETING with Shaw, Luke stopped back at the office to check in with his co-worker and buddy Ryan who was working a cold case that had come in the week before. Ryan was head down over his laptop when Luke sat down at the desk next door.

"So? How was she?"

Leave it to Ryan to get right to the point. He was definitely a man of few words, and when he did speak he tried to make it count.

"I don't know what you're talking about."

Snickering, Ryan lifted his head and swung around in his chair so he was facing Luke.

"Don't be an asshole. You went to meet a woman. We all know it. Just tell me how it went."

"What makes you think you know?"

It was a stupid game. There weren't many secrets in this office, and Luke's friends were investigators, after all.

"I heard you on the phone with your sister. And before you tell me not to listen in, you were sitting right there at your desk and I was sitting right here. I couldn't help but overhear. Shit, your voice carries. Shelly at the reception desk probably heard you."

His voice did carry. He'd had to learn to be loud to be heard in a family with a lot of kids.

"It went fine."

Luke was going to tell Ryan all the details, but he was going to make his friend work a little for it first.

"Fine? What a candy-ass word. My teeth cleaning the other day went fine. Get a thesaurus and find a better adjective."

"It was good."

Luke couldn't keep the smile from his face. This was fun. Playing with Ryan and getting him pissed off was entertaining as hell.

"I can see you trying not to laugh, you rat bastard. If you're smiling it must have been better than good or fine, for fuck's sake, so spill it. You might be bigger than me, but I can still beat the shit out of you."

Luke had three inches and about forty pounds on Ryan – who was no snowflake himself – but they were probably evenly matched when it came down to it. According to their boss Logan Wright, Ryan was an expert in hand to hand combat, plus he didn't mind playing dirty. He could be meaner than a snake if you were on the wrong side of him.

"You need to learn to chill out. Just relax, Beck. You're far too tense."

Ryan didn't reply at all, simply staring Luke down until they couldn't keep a straight face and ended up laughing.

"Seriously, I had a nice time. She's everything that Melissa promised. Beautiful, funny, intelligent. We're going to go out again."

"But?"

Luke chuckled and shook his head. "No buts. We had a great time. The date flew by. We had a lot to talk about, especially as we have the same degree in psychology."

Ryan frowned. "You're not exactly jumping for joy that you've found a woman that might be able to put up with you."

"I am, it's just…"

"Ah, here we go. What's up?"

"Her job is social media. She gives relationship advice. Not just couples, but family, friends, co-workers. That sort of stuff."

"Sounds interesting."

"I'm planning to watch some of her videos. But she has a few rather…passionate fans that are bothering her."

Ryan's brows shot up. "The plot thickens. Do go on."

Luke shrugged. "That's all I know so far. She's kept all the correspondence in a folder so I asked her to send it to me so I can look through it. Her agent has been telling her not to engage which I agree with. They've also told her that eventually he'll find someone else to bother if she doesn't give him the attention he craves. I sort of agree with that as well, although so far, he hasn't disappeared. She's blocked him numerous times apparently and he keeps coming back with a new persona."

"Persistent bastard, isn't he?"

"He is which makes me wonder if he's one of the majority that will eventually fade away on their own or one of the few that have to be persuaded."

"Did she send you the messages?"

Luke opened the lid on his laptop. "I had her email them to me. I haven't looked at them yet."

"Fire it up and I'll grab us a couple of sodas."

Ryan went into the kitchen while Luke opened up the email which had the folder attached. The messages only took a moment to load, in chronological order. Luke opened the oldest one first just as Ryan sat down, placing two cans on the desk.

They didn't speak for several minutes, silently reading the messages and then opening the next one. It was only when they were finished that anyone spoke up.

"He's escalating."

Ryan had hit the nail on the head. It was exactly what Luke had been thinking. The messages had at first started out fairly innocuous, telling Shaw how much they liked her channel, how pretty she was, how smart and intuitive, and how much she'd helped them.

That first message Shaw had replied to, which wasn't a surprise. It sounded normal and she'd already told him that she tried to answer all the messages she received – positive or negative – as long as they weren't abusive. She'd thanked the viewer and told them how much she appreciated them watching and subscribing.

Then it was off to the races.

The person took that as the opening and barraged Shaw with message after message, sometimes a dozen in one day, each one getting more bizarre and personal. Shaw must have caught on and she didn't respond back, but the man – or woman – wouldn't take no for an answer and simply created a new profile. The most recent messages had an angry and bitter tone regarding Shaw ignoring them. The last few were especially ominous, promising that she was going to regret her actions if she didn't reply.

"He is escalating," Luke agreed. "He's also getting angrier. I don't like the tone of the more recent messages."

"He might go away on his own," Ryan said in a hopeful tone. "It could happen."

Luke pointed to the screen. "If this were your sister, what would you say to her?"

Shaw was his sister's friend and that made her like family as far as he was concerned. It didn't matter whether he was dating her or not.

Ryan's lips twisted. "That she needed to watch this guy closely."

"That's what I think too. She's not going to be happy to hear that. I was hoping to be able to tell her that I looked over the messages and it was all no big deal."

"It still could be a nothing burger. We're not perfect when we make a call like this. Tighten up her cyber security and if you make it difficult enough for him, he might go away."

The question was...would Shaw let him help her? As much as he wanted to see her again, he wasn't looking forward to that conversation.

CHAPTER FIVE

"So how was your date with my brother? Tell me everything."

Melissa had stopped in after work for a glass of wine, which quickly turned into ordering a pizza for the two of them. They'd asked Taylor to join them, but she already had plans with her new guy.

"Everything?" Shaw laughed. "Are you sure? What if I slept with your brother and we had wild sex on my kitchen island? Do you still want to hear about it?"

They were sitting at Shaw's kitchen island, which had Melissa giving the offending butcher block top a nasty glare.

"You didn't, did you? Because I didn't think you were the type to jump into bed with someone. Not that there's anything wrong with that, because it would be fine, but I just sort of thought you were the slow and cautious type."

"I didn't, but you didn't know that when you asked for all the details."

"Maybe I don't need *all* the details."

Shaw shrugged. "There's nothing down and dirty to tell, I

must admit. We had coffee and shared a piece of lemon cake."

"My brother loves sweets. I bet he ate most of it."

He hadn't, so that was a point in his favor. He might have wanted to, but he didn't expect to get everything he wanted.

"It was about half and half. That's a nice little coffee shop. So we talked quite a bit about his job and my job. It was good." She gave Melissa a nudge with her elbow. "We're going out again."

Her friend did a fist pump in the air, making Shaw laugh harder.

"I knew it. I knew you two would hit it off. He's a pretty cool guy, isn't he? I mean…he's my favorite brother."

"He's your only brother."

"Even if I had a dozen, Luke would be my favorite. I know we're supposed to argue and fight, but we don't. I think he's genuinely a great guy, and he deserves to be with a nice woman."

"Thank you for the compliment. I agree that your brother is a nice man. We got along very well."

A smile played around Melissa's lips. "Admit it. You didn't expect to like him."

Sighing, Shaw had to fess up to her friend. "I didn't but was pleasantly surprised. Although, I must say that you might have warned me about how massive he is. He made the booth we sat in look like teeny-tiny doll furniture. He's huge."

Melissa nodded in agreement. "Six-four and over two-fifty. His arm is bigger around than my thigh. I guess I didn't think to mention it because it's old hat to me. Our dad is a pretty big guy too, and so is our uncle. Luckily, I took after my mother so I'm a more average height at five-five. All my sisters are except for Cassie. She's five-ten and looks like a model. Not that I'm bitter."

"It's good that you're not bitter. That would be bad."

"It would, but I'm not like that. I can let shit like that go."

"You're practically the Dalai Lama."

"I know, right?" Melissa reached for another slice of pizza. "Did you two talk about your number one fan?"

"We did."

Brows raised, Melissa wasn't going to let it go. "You did? What did he say?"

"He agreed with me that the vast majority of trolls like this go away if they don't get attention. That's another thing...you didn't mention that he and I have the exact same degree. He's a psychology nerd just like me."

"I wanted you to discover some things for yourself. Now go on, what else did he say? Serial killers and stalkers are his whole life these days."

"He asked to read the messages, so I sent them to him. He's going to look them over and then give me his professional opinion."

"What if he says that he thinks this person is dangerous?"

Shaw pushed away her empty plate and tucked her paper napkin underneath the edge.

"I'll find out what your brother thinks tomorrow night. We're going to a movie and then dinner."

Melissa looked surprised. "You didn't ask him to tell you right away? Knowing my brother he's already read those messages."

"It's not a big deal. I can wait."

"You're cooler about this than I would ever be. I'd have to know as soon as possible."

"That's me. Cool as a cucumber."

And we all know what can happen to a cucumber. They end up in a pickle.

Hopefully, that wouldn't be me.

★　★　★

LUKE PAUSED THE video he was watching when his boss Logan Wright exited his office to grab a cup of coffee. They were both there later than normal, and everyone else had gone home.

Logan frowned when he realized he wasn't alone. "I know why I'm here late, but what's your story? Don't you have two dogs waiting for you?"

Luke did have two Labradors – one yellow and one chocolate brown. Murphy and Dylan. Murphy was the clown of the duo, always having fun and making people laugh. Dylan was the introvert, far more shy but loyal to a fault once he was used to a human. He was also a cuddle bunny, lying next to Luke pretty much everywhere in the house. Murphy was far more independent, coming to get pats in between destroying his toys. Both of them were devoted to the other and they couldn't have been any closer.

"I do, but I stopped by and let them out midafternoon. They're good for a little while. They're probably taking a nap to rest up for a long walk when I get home."

They wouldn't let Luke forget, either. Murphy would grab the leash between his teeth and bring it to his daddy, laying it next to him on the floor.

Luke couldn't imagine loving them more than he already did. They had him wrapped around their furry paws.

Logan took a sip of his coffee and leaned down to look at Luke's screen. From experience, Luke knew it would be black with no cream or sugar. Practically industrial strength sludge. That's the way his boss liked it.

"What are you working on?"

Not anything that Luke had actually been assigned by the partners of this consulting firm – Logan Wright, Jason Anderson, and Jared Monroe. Nor had it been assigned by his direct supervisor Reed Mitchell. The fact was he wasn't too sure how it would be looked on that he was working on something else while in the office. He hadn't been here long enough to know.

Time to find out.

"This is a video of one of my sister Melissa's friends. She's a social media…shit, I don't even know what they call them. She basically gives relationship advice on her channel and is very successful at it. She even has a book deal. Her background is also psychology."

"I don't get a lot of this social media stuff, but it sounds interesting." Logan leaned closer. "She's pretty."

Yes, she was. Luke was already anticipating their date tomorrow night.

"She's my sister's friend."

Now why did I say that again? And in that tone?

Chuckling, Logan took another sip of his coffee. "Right. You've got no interest at all. That's why you're sitting at your desk after seven o'clock at night watching her videos. Unless you were wondering what to do about a messy roommate?"

That was the subject of the current video open on his laptop. He had been instantly impressed by Shaw's empathy but also her ability to define boundaries in a relationship. Being one of five kids, there hadn't been many of those boundaries in his home growing up. Not that he'd known any different, but he sure liked having a bathroom all to himself now.

"I had coffee with her earlier today," he finally admitted. "We're going out tomorrow night."

"I had a feeling she was more than an acquaintance," Logan laughed. "Where are you taking her?"

"A movie and then a casual dinner."

"Casual, huh? Good choice for a first date."

Should I even mention it? What the hell...why not?

"Logan, can you take a look at something for me? Give me your opinion? Ryan and I looked through these earlier, but I'd like your thoughts."

"Sure, I can do that."

Logan pulled up a chair and Luke opened the folder, letting his boss peruse the contents quietly. At one point, Luke even got up and went to get a can of soda. By the time he came back, Logan had closed the folder and was sitting back in the chair.

"You want my opinion?"

Luke nodded. "I do. What do you think?"

"How about I get to ask one question first? Are these messages to your new girlfriend?"

"They are," Luke admitted reluctantly, although he wasn't ready to characterize Shaw as his girlfriend. He'd let Logan's words pass however, as he didn't have a description that was much better. She was more than a friend but not yet his girlfriend. "I had to really work to get her to let me look at them. She's convinced it's not a big deal and that if she keeps ignoring them this person will eventually get fed up of not getting any attention and just go away."

Rising from the chair, Logan rubbed at his chin. "I don't think she's going to be that lucky, but then I'm a cynical old cop that lost his faith in humanity a hell of a long time ago. So take what I say with a grain of salt."

Everyone knew that Logan's gut was usually dead on the money.

"You going to look into this for her?" Logan asked. "Check it out?"

"Maybe this weekend—"

"Fuck that. If you need to take some time to look at this, I don't have any objections."

Shit, Luke hadn't expected his boss to let him investigate these messages. On company time.

"I couldn't ask you to let me do that. I can do this at night and on the weekends."

Logan just laughed as he headed back to his office. "We like you working at night and on the weekends too. But let me give you some advice…always err on the side of the living. Your girlfriend needs help now. So let us know what we can do to help you. Grab Ryan if you need him."

It wouldn't hurt to look a little more deeply into this. Assuming Shaw allowed him to, of course. She wasn't going to be happy, but Luke agreed with Logan. This person wasn't going to give up easily.

Luke just might need to *convince* him.

CHAPTER SIX

WORKING FROM HOME was sometimes rather isolating so Shaw made sure to leave her house and hit the gym at least three times a week. She was able to exercise and be around other human beings all at the same time. She'd never had a goal to become a hermit, but she could easily slip into that behavior if she wasn't vigilant, especially when it was cold outside or the weather sucked. It was far easier to stay home and order dinner to be delivered.

When she turned down her street the next afternoon after her workout, she had a strong urge to turn the car around and drive back the way she came. Fast.

Her mother's car was in her driveway.

What did I do in a past life to deserve this?

As far as Shaw knew, her mother and stepfather were supposed to be looking at condos today. They wanted something low maintenance and closer to town than their current home which was twenty minutes away from the nearest grocery store. They'd bought the place nine months ago because they liked their privacy. It turned out that they liked going out to dinner more.

Are they looking in my neighborhood? I might have to move.

Instantly ashamed of her thoughts, Shaw parked in her garage and took a deep breath. She loved her mother. She truly did. But…sometimes Julia Stephenson didn't make *liking* her all that easy. She'd been a difficult parent to please when Shaw was a child and it wasn't much better now.

Julia didn't like Shaw's career. Or her house. Or her neighborhood. Or her car. Or her friends. Or her shoes, or her lipstick, or any of the other hundred decisions that Shaw had made on her own. If it wasn't what Julia would have picked? It was obviously all wrong.

When Shaw entered her home, she found her mother and stepfather sitting at her kitchen island and drinking coffee as if they lived there.

I need to get that spare key back.

"Mom, Oliver, this is a surprise."

More than you can imagine.

Her mother jumped up and gave her a hug. "We were looking at houses in the Cumberland area and decided to stop by. You weren't here but we assumed you'd be home soon."

Cumberland was twenty minutes away. Not exactly close.

"I see you made yourself at home."

Julia stuck out her lower lip in a pout. "You wouldn't have wanted us to be uncomfortable, would you? That's no way to treat a guest."

Shaw didn't point out that she wasn't a host technically,

because Julia wasn't an invited guest. She didn't need to start a war with her mother. It was easier to move on to another subject.

"Did you see any condos that interested you?"

Oliver smiled and nodded. "We did. A nice three bedroom. Plenty of room if you wanted to move home."

Julia's new husband was a nice, quiet man about five years younger. Tall and wiry, he had thick brown hair that was shot with a little gray at the temples. He also had an easy smile and Shaw could see why her mother had fallen for him. He was quite the charmer.

And he'd obviously been listening to her mother because he was beating that drum again.

Move home. Not going to happen.

Should I ignore it or say something?

So far she'd just been ignoring those comments, but they hadn't gone away. As a rule she tried to avoid discussions that would upset her mother, but this was getting out of hand. Shaw was going to be thirty years old on Saturday. She'd been living on her own for years now and she had absolutely no intention of ever moving back. This was a fantasy her mother simply wouldn't let go.

"I own my home here, Oliver. I'm not sure why you would think I'd want to give it up."

"You're alone here," Julia exclaimed, retrieving a cup from the cabinet and pouring a third cup of coffee. "That cannot be healthy. You don't have anyone to look after you either. What if you get sick or hurt? You could lie here for days until someone found you."

"I text with my friends every single day. If I didn't answer they'd check on me."

"Every day?" Julia sniffed, pushing the coffee in front of Shaw. "I'm lucky to get a call once a week."

Because you make me crazy.

"You really should call your mother more," Oliver said in a reproachful tone. "She worries about you."

"You don't need to worry so much, Mom. I'm fine. Everything is fine."

"You say that but something bad could happen," her mother argued. "You need people around you that love you. Now drink your coffee."

Love me…to death.

Julia Stephenson simply didn't get it. Children were supposed to grow up and spread their wings. Make lives for themselves and become independent.

"I don't really want coffee but thank you. How about we talk about the condo that you looked at?" Shaw suggested hopefully. "What was the kitchen like? And didn't you want a big jacuzzi tub, Mom?"

Julia shrugged. "It didn't have a big bathtub, but it had a nice kitchen. Granite countertops though. I was hoping for quartz."

"We'll keep looking until we find exactly what you want, sweetheart," Oliver said with a grin, draining his cup. "If we have to look at every condo and townhouse in a five-hundred-mile radius."

Five hundred miles away? That sounded like heaven. Julia and Oliver wouldn't be dropping by unexpectedly if they lived that far.

"Now about your birthday," Julia began. "We need to make plans. That's the main reason we stopped by today."

They'd already made plans. Weeks ago.

"Did you not want to have brunch on Sunday?"

"Of course we do, but I'm your mother. Don't I get to see you on your actual birthday? You could come to our house for dinner. I'll make chicken."

Counting slowly to ten, Shaw took a steadying breath and reminded herself that she gave relationship advice for a living. She might want to take some herself.

"I already told you that I have plans on Saturday, Mom. We're going to have brunch on Sunday and then go shopping, right? It's going to be a great day."

Julia's lips pressed together. "I suppose you'll be spending Saturday with your friends."

Her mother made it sound like Shaw was planning to spend the day with Hannibal Lecter. Eating internal organs with a glass of craft beer.

"Part of it. I have other things to do as well for work."

Normally that would be Julia's cue to scoff at Shaw's idea of work. Her mother actively hated her social media career and was constantly pushing her to go back to school for her doctorate. Shaw wasn't against the idea for the future, but right now she was happy.

Instead of deriding her videos, her mother mumbled something under her breath. Oliver, bless him, kept mostly quiet for all of this. He didn't have much to say, that was for sure, which was lucky as Julia liked to be the one doing the talking. In that aspect they definitely made a great couple.

"Let me know if you change your mind. Or if your friends cancel on you at the last minute."

"I will, Mom."

It wasn't probable but there was a slim chance both Melissa and Taylor could come down with the flu. But in that case Shaw would probably have it too, along with their entire yoga class.

"Did I mention to you that Sandra's son Gerald is back in town?" Julia asked, her eyes lighting up with excitement. "He's single again. Maybe you should give him a call."

It wasn't a surprise that Gerald was single. He was a horrible human being, or at least he was the last time Shaw had seen him. He was rude, pompous, and generally unpleasant. He thought he knew everything about everything when in actuality he didn't know squat. He also thought that personal hygiene was a Madison Avenue conspiracy. Time to change the subject. Again.

"Let's talk about that kitchen that you saw today. What color were the cabinets?"

With a mother like Julia, Shaw didn't need a stalker or an online troll.

She already had one.

★   ★   ★

LUKE DIDN'T KNOW why he was nervous. This wasn't his first date with Shaw, after all. They'd both agreed that they liked each other enough to go on a second date, so she was into him. But he still wasn't calm.

It was supposed to be a casual date – a movie and then some pizza. Nothing elaborate, which they'd both heartily agreed to. Eating at some fancy restaurant with a snooty waiter wasn't their idea of fun. He was lucky that Shaw felt the same as he did. She'd even made a face when he'd suggested the elegant French place on the west side of town. It had been her idea – and a fabulous one – to grab a pizza and a movie. The film would give them something to talk about while eating the pizza if the conversation lagged.

Luke didn't anticipate that though. They hadn't had any issues at the coffee shop.

Wiping his damp palms on the denim of his jeans, he rang Shaw's doorbell and waited. For the first time in a while he was excited about spending time with a woman. He'd been thinking about her pretty much all the time since they'd met. He wanted to know more about her, her childhood, her hopes, and dreams.

Tonight he'd settle for finding out what pizza toppings she liked.

The door flew open and…Shaw looked amazing. He'd noticed that she was an incredibly attractive woman before but tonight she looked especially beautiful. Her chin length blonde hair was shiny and held back on one side with a small gold barrette. Her blue eyes were rimmed with a smoky liner and her lashes were ridiculously long and thick. She had paired a bright red sweater with dark blue jeans that made her legs look amazing. He had to remind himself to breathe before he could speak.

"Hi."

Real eloquent. He was no poet.

"Hi," she replied with a smile. "Let me get my coat and purse, okay?"

Shaw shrugged into her coat and Luke stepped forward to lend a hand as he'd been taught by his mother. She'd always drilled manners into her five children, although he had to admit that most of it hadn't really stuck until he was an adult.

Locking the door behind her, she slung her purse over her shoulder to follow him but then abruptly stopped. He followed her gaze to the house across the street. The neighbor was standing at the large picture window.

Watching.

Luke's gut immediately tightened. He didn't like this at all.

"Does he do that a lot?"

"Maybe once or twice," Shaw replied. He could hear the reluctance in her voice. "He's home quite a bit when he's not traveling, but he's really quite friendly."

"I'm friendly but I don't watch my neighbors like that." Luke scowled at the figure outlined by the lamp. "He isn't even moving or pretending he was checking the weather. He's just standing there watching us. More specifically…you. What's his name?"

"James. James Hornsby. You're going to check him out, aren't you? That's why you wanted to know his name."

"Yes, just to be safe. Someone is bothering you, Shaw. You need to be careful."

"But they're doing it online," she protested, allowing him to lead her to his vehicle and help her into the passenger seat. "James lives across the street."

"But he knows what you do?"

"Well…yes."

"So he could create profiles and send you threatening messages a hell of lot more easily than by leaving notes on your car window?"

Sighing heavily, she nodded. "I suppose you're right."

"I'm just going to check out his background. No big deal."

Luke had already planned to do it, but now Hornsby was at the top of his list. He closed Shaw's door and went around to slide into the driver's seat.

"How about we forget all about possible stalkers tonight and just enjoy the evening?" he said, wanting to diffuse the tension that had sprung up between them. He didn't want this to be about anything bad. "Deal?"

"Deal," she agreed readily, her gaze on him and not the nosy neighbor.

But as Luke backed out of her driveway and drove down the street, he could still see James Hornsby watching.

Luke was going to watch right back.

CHAPTER SEVEN

T HE MOVIE WAS one of the best Shaw had seen in a long
time. A fun murder mystery with several twists and turns,
although she'd figured out the killer about halfway into the film.
Not because she was an amazing sleuth or anything – she
wasn't – but because he was the most unlikely suspect.

"I suspected him as well," Luke said when they sat down at
the pizza place. They'd ordered a large with sausage and extra
cheese and a pitcher of ginger ale at the front counter. "The
whole character just seemed so out of place. Like why was this
big Hollywood movie star doing this small part? Oh, because
he's the killer. It only made sense at the end."

"So you didn't like the movie?"

"I loved it," Luke declared with a grin, pouring soda into her
glass. "I thought it was great, but the big reveal wasn't a huge
surprise. Now...how he pulled it off was. I loved those twists
and turns in the story and they were original. I'd see it a second
time just to see what I missed. I have a feeling that I would
notice things I didn't before."

"That's good. I was worried for a minute that you hated it. I picked it, after all."

"You did a great job, but frankly I'm easy to please. I'll watch just about anything. I love going to the movies. The whole experience with the popcorn and a soda the size of my head."

Smiling, she nodded in agreement. "I have to have my M&Ms. I mix them in with my popcorn."

"I noticed that. That's a bold move, if I may say so."

"Salty and sweet. It's the perfect combination."

"I'm going to try it next time." He paused and took a sip of his soda. "I watched some of your videos. Several of them, as a matter of fact."

Shaw buried her face in her hands. This was one of the weirder parts of her job. People watching a recording of her. She'd never get used to that.

"I'm afraid to ask what you think."

Because although she'd just met Luke Brewster, his opinion of her mattered. It shouldn't this quickly, but it did.

"I thought you were great. I can understand why you're so popular. So you can stop hiding behind your fingers. You have to know that you're good."

She dropped her hands. "I think I might be a victim of imposter syndrome."

"That's pretty common. I have it too. I keep wondering when my bosses are going to figure out that I have no fucking clue what I'm doing and I'm just making it up as I go along."

"I don't believe that. I think you know what you're doing. You have that air about you. Like everything is going to be fine and you're completely in control."

"Then I'd like my Academy Award," he laughed. "Because I've clearly fooled you and hopefully everyone I work with. Seriously, I always have my doubts about my work, but I actually think it can be a good thing. It makes me work harder and keep learning. I always want to improve."

"I feel that way too. At some point, I want to go back to school and get my doctorate. My mom has been bugging me about it lately."

Now why did I say that out loud?

"Moms can be like that," he replied with a chuckle. "They just want the best for us. My mom was worried when I went into law enforcement but now she's my biggest cheerleader."

Family dynamics had always fascinated Shaw, especially as she'd been an only child with a single mother for so long. Luke's family was wildly exotic in her view.

"Did she try and talk you out of it?"

"No, but I could tell she was worried. My sisters were worried too, but they all knew that I was determined. I'd been planning on being a cop as far back as high school." He leaned forward, his arms folded on the table in front of him. "My dad did take me aside and basically said that I needed to be sure. He asked if I'd talk to one of his friends who was a cop and of course I said yes. He didn't ask the guy to try and scare me or anything. Just the facts so I could make an informed decision."

"And you decided to become a cop. But now you're not. What made you change?"

The waitress showed up at that moment to bring their pizza, the aroma of garlic, tomatoes, and cheese making Shaw's stomach growl aggressively. The popcorn and M&Ms simply hadn't filled her up, and she absolutely adored pizza.

"I could eat this every day," Luke said, placing a few pieces on her plate before doing the same for himself. "I know that sounds terrible, but I love pizza. When I was in college, I think me and my roommates ate it about five times a week."

Shaw blew on the slice and then took an experimental bite, the savory flavors exploding on her tongue. She'd never been to this restaurant before, but Luke had assured her it was going to be delicious. He was right.

"I love it too. I also ate way too much pizza in college. Cheeseburgers too."

"I love a good cheeseburger, and I like my fries crispy. Preferably crinkle fries. What are your thoughts on fries?"

It was like they were twins separated at birth.

"I love crispy crinkle fries. I like to dip them in barbecue sauce instead of ketchup sometimes."

"Another bold culinary move. I'm going to have to try that. You're sort of a maverick in the kitchen. Tell me more."

"I eat broccoli with parmesan cheese." His brows shot up comically and Shaw couldn't hold back her laugh. "I like Swiss cheese on my hamburger instead of cheddar. I think mayonnaise was invented by the devil."

"Don't tell my mom that. She makes her tuna salad every Tuesday. And Swiss cheese on your burger? That's crazy talk, woman. It has to be American. The slices that come wrapped up like when you were kid. My dogs love them. They can hear me open a slice of cheese five miles away."

Dogs? Plural?

"You have dogs?"

He grinned and practically bounced in his chair. Clearly, he loved them because his eyes were lit up with delight. As a woman, Shaw was sure she'd never been looked at like that by a man.

"Two of them. Dylan and Murphy. Labradors. Did I not mention them before?"

"I don't think you did. I probably would have remembered two big dogs."

His smile fell and his brow wrinkled. "Uh oh, do you not like dogs?"

She had a feeling that this was a make or break question. If he had two canines, he must like them a bunch.

"I like dogs just fine," she assured him. She didn't have anything against them. "We just didn't have pets when I was growing up. But I like hanging out with my friends' dogs. Taylor has a little Yorkie named Sparkle. She's a real sweetheart. She'll sit on my lap for hours and let me pet her."

"They do bark. And they are messy. But I think it's worth it. Dylan and Murphy will also sit on your lap for hours as long as you pet them but they're significantly heavier than Sparkle. They will keep you warm on a cold winter's night though."

"You sound like a very proud dog dad."

"I am."

This man was looking better and better the more she was with him. There had to be something really wrong with him though. Melissa said that Luke was just career-focused and that's why he was single, but a guy like this should have women following him around with their tongues hanging out. Just since they'd walked into the restaurant tonight, the lady at the order counter had flirted with him and another woman across the way kept looking over and staring.

"You're almost too good to be true."

Shaw couldn't seem to control her mouth tonight.

Way to just blurt out stuff. He probably thinks you're weird.

If Luke took exception to her statement, he was good at hiding it. He only smiled and chuckled. "You want to know all my bad qualities? I can tell you, but it might be easier to ask Melissa. She's spent the better part of our lives telling me all the things that are wrong with me. How I drop my wet towels on the floor and forget to pick them up. How I like the television turned up too loud. Or how about that I don't like to leave the house once I'm home for the evening? I get comfy and don't want to move. She also hates that I like to watch football on the weekends. She thinks it's a stupid sport. I like hockey too."

Shaw took another bite of the amazing pizza. She really needed to come back here. Soon.

"Wet towels on the floor might be a deal breaker for me."

"What are your bad qualities?"

She opened her eyes wide in mock surprise. "Bad qualities? I don't have any. I'm perfect in every way."

That had him cracking up and she couldn't keep a straight face either.

"To be honest, I have so many faults I don't even know where to begin. I'm nowhere near perfect."

"Thank goodness," he said with obvious relief. "I wouldn't want to date anyone perfect. The pressure would be far too much. It's the imperfections that make us more human."

Shaw would agree with that wholeheartedly.

"What else would Melissa tell me about you? When she was trying to fix us up she only told me wonderful things."

Rubbing his chin, Luke appeared to think about the question for a moment. "She'd tell you that I work too hard and that I've hated all of her boyfriends."

"Have you hated all of her boyfriends?"

"No, but I can see why she might feel that way. I've been pretty tough on one or two of them if I didn't think they were treating her right. I didn't say anything to them because I wouldn't interfere, but I've said something to her. And only when she's asked. I told her that if she had to ask me if her guy was being disrespectful then he probably was. To be fair, she hasn't been a big fan of anyone I've dated either. She really didn't like my high school girlfriend."

Melissa hadn't mentioned any of Luke's exes and Shaw didn't want to pry...much. She was curious though.

"Why didn't she like her?"

"Melissa always says that Celia liked to be the center of attention."

Celia. Pretty name.

"Was that true?"

"Yes."

"So honest. Okay, was that an issue?"

Luke shrugged. "Not to me, but I was young back then. Celia liked the drama and at the time I didn't think anything about it. I doubt I'd enjoy that now. I like things quieter in my old age."

"Old age? You're not much older than me."

"There are days that I feel like I'm a teenager and other days like I'm a hundred. Speaking of aging…Melissa mentioned that you have a milestone birthday coming up. Is that true?"

"Saturday," Shaw confessed with a roll of her eyes. "I'm going to be thirty. We're all supposed to go out or something to celebrate. Maybe a nice meal and then dancing. I'm not sure."

Would he want to join them? So far the evening was going so well.

"You could come…you know…if you wanted to. Taylor is bringing her new boyfriend and Melissa might have a date as well."

Shaw didn't care about being the only single woman there but having Luke around could be mighty nice indeed.

His gaze was warm and she already knew his answer before he even said it. She could feel the heat crawl up her chest and into her cheeks, but it was a welcome reaction. She hadn't been this attracted to anyone in a long time. It was an unexpected surprise.

I like this. I like him.

"I'd love to come. Thank you for inviting me."

I could fall for this guy.

They'd agreed to a third date. This relationship might turn into something real. Luke Brewster was almost too good to be true.

Towels on the floor and all.

THE DATE HAD flown by and now Luke was pulling into Shaw's driveway. He couldn't remember the last time he'd enjoyed an evening so much and he was sorry to see it end. Luckily, their third date was already set up and agreed to.

Luke couldn't stop himself from glancing in the rearview mirror. Yep, the neighbor must have been waiting for Shaw to come home because he'd just pulled the curtain back, the light from his living room spilling out onto the front lawn.

I don't like this guy at all.

"Would you like to come in for a few minutes? I could make some hot chocolate."

Hell yes, Luke wanted to come in. He sure as shit didn't want to kiss Shaw in front of an audience.

"That sounds great, thank you."

He placed his hand on the small of her back as they walked to her front door. She was so small and delicate compared to him and all of his protective instincts were engaged. He shot a look over his shoulder again.

Neighbor still watching.

Shaw unlocked the door and they stepped inside. Luke walked over to her window and looked out.

"Your neighbor is absolutely monitoring you. He was waiting for you to come home and now he's still staring outside. Doesn't he have anything better to do?" Luke smiled at her. "Not that you're not fascinating – because you are – but you'd think that he might have other commitments."

Shaw slipped off her jacket and joined him, peering out into the night. The window across the street glowed, her neighbor a dark outline in the middle.

"Okay, he might be a little different. He doesn't appear to have a job, although he always has plenty of money for nice cars and vacations. I assume he's independently wealthy. I mentioned once that I worked from home and he didn't say that he did. He watches everyone in the neighborhood though, not just me. When the weather is nice, he sits on a lawn chair in his open garage and watches the cars go by."

That sounded boring as hell. When Luke had lived with his parents, there had been an old couple a few houses down and the man had done the same thing. Just sat there on his riding lawn mower, drinking a beer, and watching the world go by. But at least that made sense. He was older and he couldn't get around too well. His wife wouldn't let him actually mow the lawn anymore; their son came over to do it.

What was James Hornsby's story? It might be completely

innocent. It might not. Considering his profession, Luke was predisposed to suspect the worst, especially since Shaw lived alone.

"When did he move in? Was it about the time that you started receiving the messages?"

Shaw tugged at his arm. "No, he moved in last year. Now why don't we forget about him and relax? I'll go make the hot chocolate and you can take off your coat."

Luke didn't want to let Hornsby ruin the mood so he did as Shaw asked, shedding his coat and following her into the kitchen. The kitchen was small but well-laid out and done in shades of blue and cream. Shaw had a simmering saucepan on the stove in no time.

"Do you want marshmallows?"

"Of course, what's cocoa without marshmallows?" Luke teased. "They're the reason you drink hot chocolate. Like icing is the reason you eat cake."

"I can see you have a sweet tooth. Can you grab them out of that cabinet for me? This is ready to pour into the mugs."

A few minutes later they were cozied up on her couch, Shaw's thigh pressed against his own. He could smell the clean fresh scent of her shampoo and feel the warmth of her skin through the denim of their jeans. She looked perfectly at ease holding a Winnie the Pooh mug with her stocking feet tucked under her.

I really want to kiss this woman.

Luke held up his Tigger mug. "Is this a set? I like it."

"It is. I have Piglet and Eeyore too. I like them because they're cute and they also hold a lot. I use them for soup quite a bit." Her eyes narrowed as she looked up at him suspiciously. "Are you making fun of me, by any chance? Because I really like Winnie the Pooh."

"I am not," he vowed. "I really do like them. I also have novelty mugs at my house."

"What are yours?"

"Mostly my favorite sports teams. I do have a few that friends have given me as gag gifts. One has two Labs on it, and I use it the most. My buddy said he found it in a tourist shop in Chicago and immediately thought of me."

Her eyes widened and she sat up straight. "Wait, are your dogs okay? Do you need to get home?"

"They're fine. I fed them and took them on a long walk before I left. The television is on for company and they're probably snoozing on the couch. They can go a few hours by themselves."

"Oh, good."

Fidgeting on the couch cushion, Shaw took a sip of her hot chocolate.

"Do you want me to turn on the television? Or maybe the radio?"

She was nervous. Just as he was. He was relieved to know that he wasn't alone, and that she was feeling anxious as well.

"This is fine." Out of the corner of his eye, he spied a stack of games tucked next to the bookcase. "Do you play board games?"

Her eyes lit up. "I do. About once a month we have a game night. How about you?"

"I'm the Brewster family Monopoly champion three years running."

"That means you're cutthroat."

"You want mercy? Cry to your mama, little girl."

Laughing, she jumped up from the couch and began sifting through the boxes. "Clue? Trivial Pursuit? I'll kick your ass at that one."

"I think I heard a challenge there. Let's set it up and see who knows the most worthless facts."

An hour and a half later it was clear that Shaw was the winner. By a long shot. It wasn't even close. She knew the most bizarre stuff.

"You call me cutthroat? I've got nothing on you. You're a killer shark."

"Cry to your mama," Shaw taunted as she packed up the game. "I beat you fair and square."

Luke stood as well to help her put the pieces away, and their hands brushed accidentally. A zip of electricity ran up his arm and their gazes locked, their faces so close. He wouldn't have to lean down very far to kiss her. Mere inches.

Luke could feel her warm breath on his cheek as he leaned closer, air caught in his lungs. Her hand crept up his arm to rest on his shoulder and it was that subtle move that gave him the courage to go the rest of the way.

Their lips brushed – once and then twice – before the kiss deepened. Heart hammering in his chest, he wrapped his arms around her and pulled her closer, the heat from her body leaving a searing imprint on his own. Her lips were soft and warm, and it took all of his strength to finally end the kiss so they could both catch their breath.

Her cheeks were pink and her pupils blown wide. His shoulders rose and fell rapidly as he dragged oxygen into his starved lungs. Kissing Shaw Parker could only be compared to being hit by a truck. She was lethal and he was her willing victim.

"That was…"

He couldn't agree more.

"Yeah, it was…great."

He was such an eloquent bastard. All the blood had drained from his brain to parts farther south so he was having difficulty stringing coherent words together.

"Great," she echoed, her gaze still fixed on his lips. "It was great."

She was as dazed as he was. This was a good sign.

"I've had fun tonight," she said, moving away to place the board game back in its place. "Thank you for dinner and the movie."

That was the signal that the evening was officially over. He hadn't thought that they would end up in bed or anything so he wasn't surprised, but he had to admit that he didn't want to leave. He had images running through his head that involved a great deal of bare skin, some sweat, and crinkled sheets.

But they weren't going to do any of that. He was going to put on his coat and leave like a gentleman. Hopefully there would be other nights.

"You're welcome. I had a good time. Even if you did beat me at Trivial Pursuit. Next time we play Monopoly."

"I'm good at that too. You've been warned."

It was only slightly awkward as he shrugged into his jacket and walked to the door. It was cold outside, so he told her not to come out to his vehicle when she reached for her own coat. The two of them stood in her doorway, Shaw in her stocking feet and her arms wrapped around herself to keep warm, and him on the other side of the threshold...aching to kiss her again. Just one more time. For the road.

What the hell...

He leaned down and pressed a brief kiss to her lips and she smiled in return.

"I'll call you about Saturday," he said, brushing a stray strand of her pale blonde hair from her face and tucking it behind her ear. Her skin was warm despite the chilly temperature. "Goodnight, Shaw. Sweet dreams."

"You too. Drive carefully. There are a lot of crazy people on the roads this time of night."

"I will. I promise. Lock the door behind me, okay?"

Because there were a lot of disturbed people in this world. And one of them just might live across the street from her. He could see a strip of light from the front window where Hornsby was watching Luke leave. He heard the click of the deadbolt, and then and only then did Luke walk toward his car.

When he reached the vehicle though he didn't stop and get in. Instead, he walked across the street and stood at the end of Hornsby's driveway.

Staring right back.

I see you, asshole. I see you watching her.

The curtain immediately dropped and the front window went dark.

Go ahead, hide in the dark.

First thing tomorrow morning, Luke was going to check out James Hornsby.

He didn't trust the guy. Not one bit.

HE WAS FURIOUS. Stomping up the stairs, he locked himself in his office, pacing back and forth trying to burn off the angry energy. Shaw was pulling even further away from him. He couldn't allow that to happen. She had to learn that she belonged to him. She had to understand. How could she not see that they were meant to be together? How could she be so blind?

She hadn't left him any options.

CHAPTER EIGHT

THE SUN WAS barely up when Luke walked into the office the next morning. He wanted to get an early start so he could have some time to do a thorough background search on Hornsby. It appeared, however, that Ryan had awoken even earlier. His friend was heads down over his laptop as Luke shrugged off his coat and headed straight for the coffeemaker for his first cup.

"I made a fresh pot," Ryan called after him. "I also have what you need. You're welcome."

Taking a drink of the dark brew, Luke frowned at the file folder Ryan had dropped onto his desk. "What do you have that I need? What are you talking about?"

He hadn't had near enough caffeine yet to make heads or tails of Ryan's words.

Chuckling, Ryan sat back in his chair and stretched out his legs, propping them on the desk. "James Hornsby. You were coming into the office early to check him out. Right?"

"Yes," Luke replied cautiously. He'd sent Ryan a text last night from the movie theater after seeing Hornsby watching

Shaw. "But I'm still not following you. I haven't even had my first cup of coffee, so help me a little."

Ryan lifted up his cup. "I'm on my fourth, and I did your research for you. It was quiet and no one was here so I was able to get it done quickly."

Luke didn't know whether to thank his friend first and then ask about four cups of coffee or the other way around. His manners dictated the answer.

"Thank you. I think." He sat down and picked up the folder. "And how have you had four cups of coffee already? It's barely six-thirty in the morning. I won't have that many by lunchtime."

Ryan just shrugged. "I have an insomnia problem. I figured since I wasn't going to go back to sleep, I might as well come into the office and get some work done. I've been here since two."

"You should see a doctor about that."

"They just tell me not to drink caffeine, exercise in the morning, and don't watch television or use the computer three hours before bed. That's not going to happen. It's not a big deal. In a few days I'll fall asleep before dinner and it will all even out. Luckily I don't need much sleep."

That was a good trait to have as a cop.

"As long as you're okay with it." Luke opened the file. "Want to give me the spoilers?"

Ryan grinned at the invitation. "I'd be delighted. Your girl-friend's neighbor is a real piece of work. He comes from a super wealthy family in Seattle, but he's pretty much been thrown out as the black sheep. In college he partied so much he got kicked out of four different schools. Eventually he didn't try and go back. Life was one big party for Hornsby. All the friends money could buy. Then he got a cushy job at one of his daddy's friend's financial firms. Lost that job too. He liked to harass the pretty girls and he couldn't be bothered to show up on time or sober. He had several more jobs like that until he finally went to rehab to dry out. By that time his family had had enough. They give him an extremely generous yearly allowance on the condition that he doesn't contact them."

"His own parents basically pay him to stay away?" Luke laughed. "He sounds like a fine upstanding citizen."

"He has been for the last few years. Lives quietly and keeps to himself. Takes a vacation three to four times a year and explores exotic destinations. From what I can see he doesn't have a girlfriend, a job, many friends, or even a hobby other than traveling. The guy doesn't even mow his own lawn. He pays a service to maintain it and the house. He doesn't have a mortgage, by the way. Owns it outright. He buys a new car once a year at Christmas with cash. His last purchase was a BMW sedan. He eats mostly takeout and frozen pizzas. He does leave the house to go to the gym four times a week. He pays that membership yearly."

"You did a thorough job," Luke observed. "No stone left unturned."

"There were a few, I'm sure. I've got a few calls out to some people who might know him or his family."

"So James Hornsby is a possibly reformed asshole. Is he Shaw's troll too? Could he be harassing her online? She says that he lived there for a year before she started getting the messages."

"He doesn't have a history of stalking that I can find, although I can't get into the schools' databases. Jared might be able to. We could ask him."

Although Luke had been given permission to work on this, he wasn't sure asking one of his bosses to do some research was wise.

"I'd like to avoid pulling in others if possible."

"I thought you said that Logan told you to let him know what you needed."

"He did but I assumed that was a test."

"I don't think he would have offered if he wasn't genuine about it, but I can see your point. You don't want the guys in charge to think you can't handle a little issue that your girlfriend is having."

Luke took a sip of his coffee. "I hope this is a little issue. The fact is she could have two issues. Her online troll *and* Hornsby. He's definitely watching her all the time. Fuck, it's creepy."

"Maybe you should have a chat with him. Help him understand that Shaw isn't alone anymore."

Luke would like to, but...

"She'd kick my ass if I did that. I'd love nothing better, but Shaw wouldn't be happy. She thinks he's harmless, and even if she didn't I doubt she'd admit it. She's independent as hell."

"That's good but I hope she sees that her neighbor watching

her isn't normal."

"I think she does, but doesn't want to admit that it's weird because then she has a problem."

Luke hadn't known Shaw for long, but he could see that she liked to handle things on her own.

"So what are you going to do now?" Ryan asked.

"I'll talk to Shaw about it and try to convince her that I should confront Hornsby about his little hobby of watching her from his window. I also want to discuss her home security situation. She has deadbolts but I doubt she has anything else. Now that she's a person with a following she needs security cameras at the very least. I'm also of the opinion that she reveals too many personal details in her videos, but that's a topic for another time. I'm going to have to pick my battles carefully."

One wrong move and Shaw might kick him to the curb. He needed to tread lightly.

★　★　★

THE NEXT MORNING Shaw woke up to four new messages from her rabid online follower. A new profile. Again. The four messages were increasingly aggressive and angry. She would have described the last one as furious. They were mad that she wouldn't respond and they'd warned her that they weren't going to take being ignored lightly. Bad things were going to happen.

The warning was vague. No clear consequences were outlined but the troll told Shaw that she would be sorry if she didn't respond right away. Her fingers had hovered over the keyboard for a moment, almost hitting the reply button, but then she remembered that giving him or her attention wasn't going to get rid of them. From her studies, she knew that this person would be a bottomless bucket of need. Nothing she did would ever be enough for them. She could try and reason with him or her, but reasons were for reasonable people. Not online stalkers who demanded her personal and undivided attention.

Instead she did what she always did.

She copied the messages to her folder and then deleted and blocked the sender. This time, however, she wasn't as optimistic that this person would give up. She was beginning to think that Luke was correct in saying that her "fan" was escalating and wouldn't stop without some intervention from law enforcement. The whole situation was beginning to feel futile and a little insane. She did the same thing over and over and expected a different result.

After taking care of her daily messages and emails she padded back into the kitchen to refill her coffee cup. She paused at her front window and peeked through a small opening between the drapes. From where she was and the way the sunlight streamed in she couldn't tell if James was watching her.

Frankly, she'd made light of it last night but she'd been far more disturbed than she let on.

It creeped her out, although she was loath to admit it. The idea that he spent a good portion of his day and night watching her comings and goings was…unsettling.

He hadn't seemed strange or weird whenever she'd talked to

him in the past. He'd always been smiling and friendly. He hadn't tried to get into her house or anything. Hadn't even asked her out on a date. He'd seemed...normal.

But now these messages had her looking at everyone differently, from the barista that made her coffee to the guy that delivered her packages. Was it him? Or him? Or her? Or someone she'd never seen or met? Some stranger in another part of the country or world, sitting behind a computer and trying to make her life hell. What was the purpose? Was he trying to scare her?

I'm not frightened, but I am cautious.

Wasn't that the smart thing to be? Cautious but not let anyone change the way she lived her life. She'd given Luke permission to check out the messages. He'd also mentioned that he thought her home security was lax but until now she hadn't given it a second thought. He'd told her that since she was in the public eye she might want to install an alarm. Maybe a few cameras.

I'll talk to him about that tomorrow night.

Shaw hated to have to ask for his help, but in this case she didn't know squat about home security, and he was clearly knowledgeable. It just went against the grain to have to ask. She'd learned early and often with her mother that asking for help was basically handing over complete control.

Feeling calmer and more settled now that she had a plan, she headed back into her office to get ready to film a new video. But she couldn't stop herself from looking out her window to the house across the street.

Was he watching? Right now?

Shaw wasn't sure she really wanted to know the answer.

CHAPTER NINE

S HAW SET HER cell phone on the corner of the bathroom vanity while she finished her makeup and hair. She'd already told her mom she was in a hurry but Julia either hadn't heard or didn't care.

"I had to wish my baby girl a happy birthday."

Julia had already wished Shaw a happy birthday twice today. Once at midnight when Shaw had been dead asleep. Her mother had said that she wanted to be the *first* to wish her a happy birthday. Then she'd called again in the morning while Shaw was eating breakfast. Both times Julia had mentioned how sad it was that she wasn't going to get to actually *see* her daughter on the anniversary of her birth.

Basically, Julia was packing Shaw's bags for a guilt trip.

I didn't rise to the bait. This time, anyway.

"Thank you again, Mom. It's been a nice day."

"I wouldn't know but I'll take your word for it. Are you going to be out late tonight celebrating with your friends?"

The way her mother said the word *friends* was the same way Shaw said *politicians*.

"It will be fine."

Anything after ten was late to Julia when it came to her daughter. High school had been particularly challenging.

"So we're meeting for brunch at ten-thirty?"

"Eleven, Mom. I made the reservations for eleven."

They'd already talked this subject to death. All this meant was that Julia and Oliver were going to be incredibly early and they would talk about how Shaw had been "late" for her own birthday brunch for the next several months.

"Oh, right. Eleven. Well, I guess we'll see you tomorrow then."

Ten minutes later Shaw was able to extricate herself from the conversation and get on with her makeup. She wanted to look good tonight. Not just because she was turning thirty and it was a milestone. She was ready to admit that she wanted to look good for Luke.

I'm completely smitten.

He'd sent her a text this morning wishing her a happy birthday and then a few hours later a bouquet of flowers and a box of her favorite chocolates had shown up at her front door. Clearly, he'd talked to his sister about the gift because the flowers had been her favorite too. That he'd gone to that much trouble had her feeling all warm inside. Could he really be as wonderful as he appeared? Was there something terribly wrong with him but he was an expert at hiding it? Melissa had said that he was single because of his career, which Shaw understood. She was dedicated as well, but Luke was so handsome and sweet he should have women following him around wherever he went.

She finished up her lipstick just as the doorbell rang. Luke. Her heart accelerated in her chest and she had to make a concerted effort to take a deep breath. Even her palms were sweating. This was a guy she could fall for. Maybe. If she let herself.

If he was what he appeared to be. She'd been burned in the past. Her last boyfriend had seemed outwardly fine but eventually she'd seen that emotionally he was a mess. Clingy, whiny, and immature.

The man on the other side of her front door, however, wasn't any of those things. He was breathtakingly handsome, looking especially yummy tonight. Dressed in khaki slacks and a black sweater, he was tall and fit and damn, he even smelled great. She breathed in a lungful of his warm scent as she stepped back to let him in the house. It was then that she realized he had been holding a package behind his back.

A present?

Leaning down to drop a kiss on her lips, he then held out the brightly wrapped package with a large purple bow.

"Happy birthday."

Surprised, Shaw accepted the package. "I don't know what to say. You already sent me flowers and candy."

Luke grinned and ran a fingertip over one of the loops of the bow. "But you didn't get to open those. Everyone should have a gift to open on their birthday. So go ahead. Open it."

I do love to open presents.

The box wasn't huge, but it wasn't small either. So it wasn't jewelry and it wasn't a new coat. Other than that she didn't have a clue.

She gave it a little shake but there wasn't a rattling sound. It sounded…silent. It didn't make any noise at all. Sneaking a peek at Luke, he was still just standing there patiently waiting for her to open the gift. It shouldn't have felt awkward but it kind of did. They hadn't known one another for very long and now he'd purchased something for her that wasn't generic like flowers. This was personal. It was a test of sorts.

Sliding her finger under a corner of the paper, she pushed open the end of the package, careful not to rip or wrinkle the pastel wrapping.

Luke groaned and then grinned. "You're one of those. The kind that say things like *please save the bow* and *don't tear the paper.*"

Giggling, she gave him a mean look. "I suppose you're the kind that just dives in and rips them all open in five minutes on Christmas morning."

"Damn straight. Proud of it too. If you ask my mom, she'll tell you that I have a zest for living. At least that's what she told my school principal."

Shaw's mind was officially in the gutter. She couldn't stop herself from wondering about what else he had a zest for. Would he dive into his partner that enthusiastically in the bedroom? It was a heady thought.

The wrapping paper was discarded onto her foyer table,

leaving a plain black box. She opened the lid and folded back the delicate tissue paper…

A sweater. But not just any sweater. It was a beautiful cream-colored cardigan that she'd been eyeing when shopping with Melissa and Taylor. She'd talked herself out of it because technically she didn't *need* another cardigan, no matter how soft and pretty.

"You asked Melissa."

"I checked with her," he confirmed. "I didn't want to get you something you hated and we haven't known each other that long. Frankly, for all I knew you were allergic to flowers and hated chocolate."

"I like flowers and I love chocolate." Her cheeks were pink with warmth and she tugged at his sleeve to pull him down for a kiss. He tasted like toothpaste so he must have just brushed his teeth. Another point in his favor. "And I love this sweater. Thank you so much."

"You're welcome, birthday girl."

Their gazes locked for a long moment and the whole world seemed to melt away as she lost herself in his blue-gray eyes. An awareness shimmered between them almost palpable enough to see and feel. She had a terrible urge to forget all about her friends waiting at the restaurant. She could drag Luke back to her bedroom and have her wicked way with him. But she wasn't the type to blow off her friends…

But I might be the type to drag him into a bedroom. Later.

Straightening, he cleared his throat and tugged at the collar of his sweater as if overheated. She was feeling rather toasty at the moment as well. There was definitely some heat between them. Perhaps tonight would be the night to explore it?

Let's see where the evening takes us.

★ ★ ★

A DELICIOUS DINNER had been consumed, Shaw had blown the candles out on her birthday cake, and she'd opened her gifts from Melissa and Taylor. After dinner they'd moved the party to a small nightclub that wasn't too loud or rowdy, mostly filled with an older crowd who wanted to dance and enjoy a few cocktails.

"You and Shaw look very cozy tonight," Melissa observed when Shaw, Taylor, and Taylor's new boyfriend Austin were talking about the state of social media and its influence on young people. "I take it things are going well? You're welcome."

Luke rolled his eyes. "If I haven't thanked you then…thank you. It is going well so far."

"I was right."

"And you were right," he sighed. "Happy now?"

"Incredibly. Seriously though, I'm glad to see you two together. After that loser Shaw dated a few months ago, she deserved someone more stable in her life that would appreciate her."

Warning bells went off in Luke's head. "You never mentioned an ex-boyfriend."

"She's a young woman, bro. Did you think she hadn't dated

anyone before you?"

"Of course not, but you make him sound a little unstable."

Melissa blew out a long breath. "He kind of was. He was so controlling and needy. He didn't like her to hang out with her friends and he had to know where she was all the time. He'd text her like twenty times while we'd be in the movie theater even though she'd told him that we were going to a movie. We'd be having a cocktail, you know, just the girls, and all of the sudden he'd show up acting like he was just in the neighborhood. He thought every guy in the universe was after her and he didn't like her talking to anyone. He was also whiny and if she didn't give him enough attention he'd throw a tantrum like a toddler, trying to guilt her into doing whatever it was he wanted her to do. That went on for about two months and then she dumped him."

Those warning bells were practically exploding in Luke's ears.

"How did he take the breakup?"

She shrugged. "Not well at first. He hounded her until he realized that she wasn't going to change her mind."

"And it never occurred to you that her ex-boyfriend could be one and the same with her online troll?"

His sister's eyes widened and her mouth fell open in surprise. "Shit, no. I mean, I didn't put the two together. He seemed to go quiet, so I didn't think. Aw, fuck."

Luke patted his sister's hand. "It's not a big deal. There's probably not a connection but I think I should check it out."

"Did you check out her neighbor? James, I think? He's a

strange one. Whenever Taylor and I are there he sort of hangs out in his yard until we walk outside. Then he runs over and tries to talk to Shaw. He gives me the creeps."

Hornsby gave Luke the creeps as well.

"I have and he has an interesting background. I'm keeping my eye on him. I want Shaw to upgrade the security of her home."

Melissa didn't have the chance to reply as Shaw turned back to him when a new song started to play. "I love this song. Will you dance with me?"

A beautiful woman wanted him to hold her in his arms to the beat of a slow ballad?

Fuck, yes.

The beat was soft and sensual, and they melded together as if they'd been partners their whole lives. Luke wasn't the most graceful of men, considering his size and all, but he had enough rhythm not to embarrass himself. Shaw, on the other hand, moved effortlessly, her body brushing his over and over again until he was almost crazy with want. From the mischievous smile playing on her lips, he had a pretty good idea that she knew exactly what she was doing.

Two could play at that game.

He glided his hand from the middle of her back to her hip, his fingers insinuating themselves in the gap between the waistband of her jeans and her sweater, just slightly brushing the warm flesh. He didn't imagine her quick indrawn breath or the way her pink tongue darted out and licked her full lips.

His own heart was pounding against his ribs and he had to fight every instinct that was swelling up inside of him not to lift her into his arms and carry her out of this nightclub, going straight to her home and ravishing her for the better part of the night. Although he'd gladly do it if she gave him any indication that she wanted him to. But he'd need more than a few sweet sighs to be sure.

Experimentally, he slid his hand up her spine to the fragrant spot beneath her ear and stroked the satin skin. As he'd hoped, she shuddered and her forehead nestled against his chest more closely. If they'd been alone, he would have pressed a kiss to her neck but they had an audience. He didn't mind a little PDA but this was practically foreplay. That was private.

Sadly, the song ended and he had to take a step back, instantly missing the warmth of her body close to his. Holding her hand, they joined the rest of the group at the table. With a grimace, Melissa held up Shaw's phone.

"It's been going off for the last five minutes," she said, brows pulled together. "We didn't want to bother you but they keep calling back."

Shaw accepted the cell and then sighed. "It's my mother. I should call her back."

Luke wasn't sure what was going on but a look passed between Melissa and Shaw, one that he couldn't quite decipher. He only knew that it wasn't a happy one. Shaw didn't appear to be happy that her mother had called, which seemed strange to him. He would have loved talking to his mom on his birthday, but he was old enough to realize that not everyone had a good relationship with their family.

He wanted to give her the space to deal with this. Perhaps she'd tell him later what was going on.

"Why don't I go up to the bar and get us another round?" he suggested. "Austin, want to give me a hand?"

Taylor's boyfriend grinned and jumped up from the booth. "That's a great idea. What would you ladies like?"

They all gave their orders and the men headed to the bar, shouldering their way through the milling crowd.

"So you're a cop?"

Luke chuckled at Austin's question. He got this one all the time, so he had his answer down pat by now.

"I used to be. Now I'm a law enforcement consultant. We work with small police offices that may not have the manpower for difficult cases."

"Like murder?"

"Like murder." Luke leaned over the bar and gave the bartender their order. "What about you?"

"I'm in finance. Mergers and acquisitions. Tons of hours but it pays great."

The conversation lagged at that point. They really didn't know each other and while they might have a lot in common, they weren't going to find out standing at a crowded bar waiting for cocktails to be made.

Glancing over his shoulder, Luke saw that Shaw was off the phone but now two guys were standing at the booth. Standing close. Too close. Melissa was frowning and trying to lean back as one of the men leaned down so that his face was only inches from hers. Knowing his sister – and he did – the guy might want to be careful. Melissa had a mean right hook. He'd taught it to her and he was damn proud of how well she'd learned.

"Grab those two drinks," Luke said, taking three of them in his hands. "Looks like the ladies have company."

At first it seemed like Austin didn't understand, but then his confused expression cleared and he groaned. "We'd barely even stepped away. They must have been watching for an opening."

Luke shrugged. "They're beautiful women."

As a big guy, he didn't get into many altercations with other people. Usually all he had to do was stand next to someone and that was enough to make them go away. So he wasn't planning on being an asshole to these guys tonight. Hopefully once they realized that the ladies weren't interested, they'd get the message and go.

"Here you are," he said, placing Shaw's soda down, then Melissa's and Taylor's. It wasn't easy because the two guys didn't budge an inch and Luke had to step around them. He didn't give them any attention, simply pretending that they weren't there.

"Hey, we were talking to the girls," one of them said before turning around to face Luke. His eyes widened as he looked up – way up. He was easily eight or nine inches shorter. "Man, we didn't realize they were here with anyone. Sorry."

He grabbed his friend who smelled like a brewery, and they

stumbled away, lost in the crowd near the bar. Luke slid in next to Shaw and Austin sat down next to Taylor.

Melissa rolled her eyes. "Thanks, big brother. They were becoming obnoxious."

Austin chuckled and took a drink of his soda. "I helped too, you know. They were clearly intimidated by Luke's size and my scorching intellect."

Taylor placed her arm around Austin and gave him a peck on the cheek. "My hero."

Shaw, however, was strangely quiet. She was scowling and still holding her phone.

"You okay?" He glanced down at the cell phone in her hand. "Bad news?"

"No."

"Why don't we all go out and dance again?" Melissa asked loudly, clasping her hands together. "I like this song."

Luke flicked a glance at his sister, whose gaze was darting back and forth between himself and Shaw. What had happened while he'd been gone?

"That sounds like a great idea," Luke agreed. "How about it, Shaw?"

She shook her head. "I don't want to dance."

That was fine too.

"I'm tired," Shaw announced. "I just want to go home."

"I can drive you home. If you're sure."

"I'm sure. Let's go. I'm getting a nasty headache."

The birthday party was clearly over. Austin and Taylor

quickly left as he had to be up early in the morning. Luke waited while Melissa and Shaw went to the ladies' room and then walked them out to his vehicle. His sister had left her car at the restaurant, so he drove the three of them there. No one said much other than to remark about how much the temperature had dropped in the last few hours. Shaw and Melissa hugged, and Luke was sure he heard an *I'm sorry* whispered between them.

"Text me when you get home?" he asked his sister as she unlocked the car doors. "So I know you're okay."

"Of course, big brother. I'll shoot you a text the minute I get home." Melissa glanced over to where Shaw was standing. "Good luck."

"I'm going to need it."

"It will be fine. We'll talk tomorrow."

He waited until his sister drove away, the red taillights fading into the distance.

Luke had a feeling that this was going to be an extremely quiet and tense drive home.

CHAPTER TEN

S HAW FIDDLED WITH the straps of her purse as she and Luke drove toward her home. She was miserable and it was her birthday. Those two things shouldn't be allowed together but here she was.

She only had herself to blame. She'd let her mother get under her skin. Again. She talked a big game about boundaries to her subscribers but in the end, she was a gigantic wuss. To make it worse, she'd ruined Luke's night too. He didn't deserve this. He'd gone out of his way to make the evening special.

"I'm sorry about tonight."

"I am too, honey. I just wanted you to have a nice birthday."

"I did. It was. I just…I'm really sorry."

"It's fine. No worries. It's you I'm worried about. Do you want to talk about it?"

"Do I? Not really, but you deserve an explanation."

"You don't have to talk about it if you don't want to." He paused, as if wondering whether to keep talking. He must have decided the answer was yes. "I did notice that your demeanor changed after your mother called."

"My mother is…difficult at the best of times."

"Family can be that way."

From what Melissa had said describing her upbringing, Luke really didn't get what she was saying. The Brewsters were practically The Brady Bunch.

"Let's just say that my mother has made an art out of trying to control everything and everyone around her. Including me."

He whistled under his breath. "That sounds exhausting for her. She must be frustrated pretty much all the damn time, I would imagine."

Luke had summed up Shaw's mother perfectly.

"She is but that hasn't stopped her. She still tries to control me and that makes our relationship harder than it needs to be."

"So when she called it wasn't to wish you a happy birthday?"

Shaw sighed and rolled her eyes. "She's already done that three times today. Call number one was at midnight so she could be the first person to wish me a happy birthday. Then she called me in the morning and then in the early evening when I was getting ready. She's upset that she won't see me until tomorrow, completely ignoring the fact that I'm planning to spend the whole day with her."

The sentence had come out in a testy tone that Shaw wasn't happy about. She shouldn't let her mother get to her like this.

"Midnight?" Luke chuckled. "Does she do that every year?"

"Not every year, but when I *disappoint* her she will. She's upset that I'm spending my birthday with my friends instead of her. And yes, I realize how ironic this entire situation is because I don't take my own advice."

"What would your advice be to someone else?"

"The usual. Set boundaries. Don't back down. Be calm and matter of fact and don't rise to the bait."

"You rise to the bait?"

"Almost every damn time. I don't know what it is, but I find myself falling into her guilt traps constantly. It doesn't help that she was a single mother raising me. My dad ran off with his assistant when my mom was pregnant and I've never met him, so it was just me and her for my entire childhood. She remarried last year though, and I thought it might mean that she'd step out of my life a little bit."

"But that didn't happen?"

Shaw shook her head in frustration. "Not at all. If anything, she's got Oliver on her side too. They're looking for condos and they want to get a three bedroom in case I want to move home. That's what he said. I was like why would I want to move home when I have my own house? It doesn't make any sense at all except to them."

"They want you to move in with them? And they're newly-weds? That's…interesting."

"It's insane."

"My parents love us, but I think they were really thrilled to get their house and privacy back when we all moved out. They turned my old room into an office for my dad."

"I can only dream of a parent like that."

"It could be worse."

Really?

"How could it be worse?"

"You might not have the introspection to realize that you're being manipulated."

"I realize it but I don't push back."

"It sounds like you do, but your mother doesn't like it. She may never change how she reacts. You know as well as I do that you can only change how *you* react. But cut yourself some slack. It's not easy to put up boundaries with people we love. She's your mother and that has its own emotional stakes built in. I think you're doing fine."

He did? He was being nicer than she was to herself.

"You haven't known me long."

"True," he conceded. "But I think you may be too hard on yourself. Your mother has had thirty years to learn exactly what buttons to push. By now, she's an expert."

"I think it comes naturally to her."

"At this point in her life, it probably does. She may not even be aware she's doing it. It's just become the way you two communicate."

"I don't want it to be like this, but when I try to talk to her she cries and gets upset. She says I don't love her."

"You said it yourself. She's manipulating you. Do you truly think that she believes that you don't love her?"

Sometimes…I don't. Wait. I do love her, but I don't always like her.

"She's convincing."

Luke pulled into Shaw's driveway and killed the engine. "I'll walk you to your door and make sure you get inside okay."

She liked his protective instincts. She wasn't of the opinion that she needed them, but it was nice that he cared.

"Why don't you come in for some hot chocolate? I feel like I cut our evening short at the club. It's still early. We could play a game and maybe I'll even let you win this time."

"Fighting words," he chuckled. "And I'll take that challenge. Prepare to be vanquished."

"You'll be crying to your mama before the night is done," Shaw taunted as she gave him her hand so he could help her out of the car. It was a chilly evening and she pulled her coat more closely around her neck before glancing over her shoulder. More specifically, across the street. The house was dark. "He must be asleep or out with friends. I haven't seen him all day."

"Good. Maybe he's found another hobby besides watching you. But I doubt it. This is probably just a short reprieve. Perhaps he has the flu."

As creepy as it was for a neighbor to watch her so closely, she didn't want James to be sick either.

"Maybe he went out of town again," she suggested, unlocking the front door. The lamp she'd left on in the living room shone reassuringly as they both entered the much warmer house. "He travels quite a bit."

They dumped their coats on the back of a chair along with her purse, and she led Luke into the kitchen.

"Do you want marsh—"

The question died in her throat when she flipped on the kitchen overhead light. A small birthday cake was sitting on her table. A card next to it. The candles were lit.

And they hadn't burned down all that far.

Someone had been in her house.

★　★　★

IT WAS A complete clusterfuck of unimaginable proportions. Shaw was upset and in tears, rightfully so, but that had made it more difficult for him to get the answers to the questions he desperately needed. He didn't want to overreact, but he didn't want to underreact either.

"Are you sure it wasn't your mother?"

"No, she's at home with her husband."

They'd opened the card carefully. Luke had made her use a tissue in case there were prints on it.

"This is definitely not my mother."

The card wasn't signed but it sounded just like her not-so-friendly online troll. He'd used the same words and style. As predicted...

He'd escalated.

"He's been in my house, Luke. My home. He knows where I live."

Luke was furious about the whole situation. Once they'd eliminated Shaw's mother or any of her friends, they'd called the police to report a break-in. He'd marched Shaw back out of the house and into his car to wait for the cops to arrive. Normally he would have checked out the house himself, but he wasn't carrying a firearm and she was so upset he didn't want to leave her alone.

The police had eventually arrived and Luke had greeted them, giving the officer in charge his business card, and letting them know that Shaw was a public figure who had been harassed online by a so-called fan.

Clearly, from their actions they didn't give a shit. Shaw lived in a small town outside of Seattle and King County. He didn't expect the cops to have a great deal of experience with a stalker, but it appeared that they didn't have any at all.

They asked Shaw some questions, mostly about her love life, which was all well and good because Luke wanted to talk to her latest ex as well, but they didn't seem to pursue any other line of investigation. They didn't check outside for footprints. They didn't care about fingerprints or DNA off the envelope. They didn't want to see the folder of messages she'd previously received. The officer in charge kept assuring her that it had to be one of her friends because there was no sign of forced entry. Who all had a key?

Shaw, her mother, and Melissa. That's it.

Luke assured the officer that his sister had been with them earlier this evening and that there was no way she did this. To prove it, he texted Melissa and asked her, showing the reply to the cop.

He was ready to tear his hair out when his boss Logan Wright walked in the door. What in the hell?

"What are you doing here? How did you get by the cops? This is a crime scene."

Logan's brows rose. "Do they know that? Because there's no yellow tape and I just walked up and into the house. As for what I'm doing here, you did give your business card to the officer in charge, right?"

"I did."

"He called me to let me know that if you interfere in their investigation he's going to arrest you. He wanted me to warn you. So here I am. Warning you."

From the smirk on Logan's face, he wasn't taking the warning any more seriously than Luke did. As in *not at all*.

"What investigation? They've asked a few questions and then tromped all over the crime scene. If we could have gotten any evidence, it's all fucked up now."

"They're not taking this seriously?"

"Not from what I can see but I might be biased."

"In other words, they're not doing what you would?"

"Exactly." Luke rubbed at his aching temple where a headache was beginning to bloom. "Jesus, let me introduce you to Shaw."

Shaw was sitting only a few feet away on the couch where the officer was asking her the same questions again. She must have answered them the same as well because he was walking away to talk with one of his other men.

"Shaw, this is my boss Logan Wright. Logan, this is Shaw Parker."

They shook hands and Logan took the seat that had been vacated by the cop. "It sounds like you've had one hell of a birthday, Ms. Parker. I'm sorry that this has happened to you."

"I'm sorry, too." She gave him a watery smile but then it turned into a frown. "Forgive me, but…how did you know?"

Logan nodded toward the officer. "Luke gave the officer his business card and they called me."

"Oh." She blinked in confusion. "Do they want you to help?"

Smiling, Logan shook his head. "That would be a definite no. They're quite adamant that they can handle this. On the other hand, Ms. Parker, you have the right as a citizen to hire a private investigation firm if you wish."

"I wouldn't even know where to begin with something like that."

"I might be able to make some recommendations."

What was my boss talking about? He was going to hand this case over to someone else?

"In the meantime, do you have a place to stay tonight?"

"She can stay with me," Luke said firmly. "That's not a problem."

Shaw's front teeth were sunk deeply into her bottom lip. "I could call my mom…or Melissa…"

She didn't sound like she wanted to call her mother. Not to Luke. He could take her to Melissa's place if that's what she wanted. His sister was wide awake after his call and pacing the floor waiting for more information.

"I'd really like it if you stayed with me."

He was ready to get smacked down but he couldn't stop from saying the words. He'd only known this woman a short time but everything inside of him was screaming in his head to protect her.

"Yes."

Just one simple word. But it changed everything.

It changed *them*.

CHAPTER ELEVEN

T HE ONLY WORD that could sum up Shaw's feelings at the moment was *violated.*

That's how she felt more at this moment than at any point in her life. Some unknown person had come into her home while she wasn't there. They might have rifled through her belongings, touching personal items. She didn't like the feeling at all, and that's why she was in Luke's shower trying to scrub away the dirty feeling that hung over her since she'd found that cake on her kitchen counter.

There simply wasn't enough soap to get rid of the icky emotions, however, so she eventually stepped out of the shower and into a pair of flannel pajama pants and an old oversized sweatshirt. Her hair was damp at the ends and her face had been scrubbed clean of any trace of makeup. When she looked in the mirror, she basically looked the same but she didn't feel it. Her life had been turned upside down.

She'd been so arrogant to think that she couldn't be touched by something like this – naive too – which was a laugh and a half because as someone who had studied human psychology, she should have been more prepared for this.

I should have known.

Was it her optimistic nature that made her assume that everyone and everything were going to be all fine and dandy? In her job, she heard really terrible problems. People were in real pain. Had she been giving them her best? She wasn't so sure now. Perhaps she had been too glib, too rosy in her advice. Some situations were fucked up and this was one of them, but she was sure she was far from alone. People went through bad crap every day. This was simply her turn.

One thing was for sure. She was going to be different when doing her job now.

Placing her towel in the hamper Luke had pointed out, she padded into the kitchen on sock feet to find him dressed just as casually and stirring a pan of something on the stove. The two dogs she'd been briefly introduced to when she arrived immediately jumped to attention, their brown eyes gazing at her even as they squirmed in their seated positions.

"They want to run up and greet you, but I haven't told them they can move yet."

Luke did seem to have trained his canine companions well. When he'd opened the door they'd practically ran him over with their excitement, but when they'd realized that he wasn't alone they were beside themselves with joy.

A new human! Yay! Let's smell her and give her kisses!

He wasn't having any of that. He'd quickly said their names in a stern voice and then told them to *sit.*

Heck, I almost sat down too.

Two furry bottoms had hit the floor, tails wagging excitedly and tongues lolling out. They'd even stayed there as he gave her a tour of the house and led her into the bathroom where she could get comfortable. There had been a few whines and one lone bark, but they hadn't moved.

He turned from the stove, setting the pan on a potholder on the counter. "I made us some hot chocolate since we didn't get any before. I thought the heated milk might help you sleep."

"I'm not sure if I could keep anything down. Honestly, I'm not sure if I'll sleep at all. I don't want to close my eyes."

Because then she kept seeing that creepy birthday cake.

With a tentative hand, she reached out and stroked one of the dog's ears. It whined and nuzzled her hand with its nose, trying to get more affection.

"Are you okay with them? I can tell them to go lie down if you want me to."

They were looking at her with such love and longing there was no way she could banish them to the two large cushions in the corner of the living room. That was far too cruel. Their tails were wagging a mile a minute and they looked like they wanted to jump out of their fur coats.

"I like dogs. I'm just not around them very much."

"Well, they're friendly as hell. They might lick you to death if you're not careful. They love people."

They certainly did. Shaw sat down on the tile floor and petted the dogs, letting them shower her with affection for several minutes.

It helped. Their complete and total adoration was like a balm to her shattered soul and she allowed herself to luxuriate in it, all the while knowing it was only temporary. Eventually she'd have to stand up and deal with the mess that was currently her life.

Luke held out his hand to help her up from the floor. "Cold noses and warm paws. The perfect antidote to a shitty day."

"They do help." She accepted the steaming mug and let him lead her into the living room. "I'm not sure how I'm supposed to feel."

They settled onto the couch next to one another, the dogs at their feet. It was only then as she sipped her hot chocolate that she really noticed her surroundings.

This was Luke's home. They hadn't known one another long so she wasn't sure what she had expected but this wasn't it. Okay, maybe she had expected a sixty-inch flat screen and sports memorabilia all over, but that wasn't what she was seeing. There were throw pillows, a colorful afghan draped over the back of a chair, and floor to ceiling drapes that pooled at the bottom.

Yes, there was a television but it wasn't any larger than her own. The only real stereotypical bachelor item was the leather recliner with a small table next to it with the remote. If she'd been shown a picture of this living room, she never would have thought he lived there.

"How do you feel?" he asked. "I would imagine that there's no right way to deal with something like this. If you want to scream you can, although my neighbors might call the cops.

They can be a bit nosy. If I work too many long hours, my neighbor kitty-corner drops off a tray of lasagna so I won't starve."

I just bet she does.

"She probably likes you. She might want to go out with you."

"Alice? She's about eighty and tells me these wild stories about when she and her late husband Earl used to swing with the other couples in their neighborhood back in the '70s. Not this neighborhood, by the way. I don't think she'd want to date me. I'm too conservative for her. She makes a damn fine lasagna, though. A nice strawberrry and rhubarb pie too."

"I think you just might be spoiled," Shaw observed. "All the women in your life want to do things for you."

His eyes twinkled at her statement. "You think so? What are all of these females doing for me, pray tell?"

She let her gaze wander around the room. "I bet they decorated your house, for starters."

Laughing, Luke nodded in agreement. "My sisters did this. I would never have picked out half of this stuff, but they said it was important. It's nice but I'm not up on the latest in home decor. I trust them for that."

"It is nice."

He rubbed his stubbled chin. "If you don't want to talk about what happened tonight we don't have to."

"No, it's fine. It's just that I'm sort of numb. I feel so violated and I keep expecting this huge wave of anger to well up inside of me and then I'll do that screaming that you suggested, but I don't feel any of that. I feel…exhausted. Like I just ran a marathon. I want to curl up and sleep for a million years but intellectually, I know that's my brain trying to shut everything off and push it away so I don't have to deal with it. Eventually I'll have to wake up and get out of bed, right? This is so crazy because I want to rest but there's no way in hell that I'm going to sleep tonight. Absolutely no way."

"You don't have to sleep if you don't want to. We can stay up all night playing Monopoly…or any other board game. Or we can watch television, or the pups will let you throw that ball right there over and over and over again until your arm falls off. Whatever you want to do."

Shaw didn't know what she wanted to do. Except…

"I think that I want to talk about it," she finally said. "If I talk out loud it might help me try to make sense of this in my brain."

"Then we'll talk about it."

There was an uncomfortable silence that followed until she realized he was waiting for her to start. Okay…here it goes. She started with the first question off the top of her head.

"How do you think he got into my home? I'm sure that the door was locked when I left and when we returned."

Strumming his bottom lip with this thumb, he contemplated her question. "I've been thinking about that myself. Since those asshole cops wouldn't let me walk around your house and investigate, I can only give you some theories."

He didn't sound happy. In fact, he'd growled that last sentence and his eyes had gone an icy gray.

"They pissed you off."

She didn't phrase it as a question because it wasn't one. It was clear he was mad.

"They did," he confirmed. "I get their point of view. There was no forced entry – at least that's what they say. It's your birthday so someone could have genuinely tried to surprise you. Also, they might be putting this down to a jealous ex-boyfriend since I was there. They were probably frustrated as well because there wasn't much they could do for you. They couldn't give you a restraining order because they don't know who did this. All they could do is make a report and tell you to be watchful and careful."

"But you think they should have done more."

"Yes," he growled again. "They could have tried to get prints and DNA from the envelope and card. They could have looked for tracks outside the house and maybe found a shoeprint. They could ask the neighbors for any surveillance footage they might have. They could also grab traffic camera footage from the nearest red light. They could have offered to try and find the IP address of those messages. They didn't do any of that."

Shaw opened her mouth to respond but she didn't get the chance. Luke wasn't done.

"If they were really motivated, they'd find out about your daily routines. Who delivers your mail, makes your coffee? Who sees you on a regular basis? They'd check them all out. They'd also tell you to get some goddamn home security instead of saying that you should be careful and watchful. Fuck, you need security cameras installed around your home inside and out, plus an alarm system. Then the next time your *number one fan* comes sniffing around he'll get a big surprise."

He didn't have to say that if she'd had a security camera there would be no questions as to whether it was a friend that had been in her home tonight. Melissa and Taylor had both suggested that she at least get a doorbell camera months ago but she'd been adamant that she didn't need it.

She'd been wrong.

"I see you have some strong feelings about the abilities of the cops at my house."

Sighing, he rubbed at the back of his neck. "I get it. I really do. These small community sheriff offices are understaffed and underfunded. They don't have the budget to have a forensics team. They don't routinely look for DNA unless someone has been murdered or assaulted. They don't deal with cyber security and they sure as hell don't have the resources to follow you around for a day or two and figure out who you come into contact with on a day-to-day basis. That's why my bosses put together their firm. They wanted to help."

"But these police don't want your help?"

"They don't. They just want your issue to go away, and most of the time it does, but I don't think this guy is planning on that. He's getting bolder and he's moving closer."

Was that code for wanting to get closer to *her*? She had a

feeling it was.

"To me?"

"Yes. To you." He reached out and placed his hand on her shoulder, his strong finger massaging the stress-knotted muscles. She closed her eyes and tried to relax and enjoy the attention. Luke was doing everything he could to take care of her. "As for how he got into the house I don't think he came in through the front door. So many people now have doorbell cameras, I doubt he would chance it. I think he came through either the back door or a window."

Once again, the thought of someone in her home made her shudder with revulsion.

"How did he time it just right? The candles were barely burned down."

"Now that I don't know. Yet. He might have just been lucky."

"If we'd come home earlier—"

"Don't even think about that. I would have been with you and nothing would have happened. I wouldn't have let him hurt you."

She believed that. Even now she felt safe and protected when he was sitting beside her. He made her feel like he had it all under control.

Which it wasn't. It was all shit but for the most part his calm and strong demeanor had kept her from losing her mind these last few hours.

"We're assuming it's a him. It could be a her."

"That's true."

Shaw's gaze settled on the closed drapes over the front window. It was almost just like the one in her home. "You suspect James?"

"As far as I'm concerned, everyone in your life is a suspect until they've been ruled out."

"I think we can safely say that Melissa, Taylor, and Austin aren't guilty. They were with us tonight."

His lips quirked up in a half-smile. "You could, but I would argue that since we had to drop Melissa off at her car and then took a few minutes saying goodbye that Taylor and Austin had time to drive over here, get into your apartment, and leave the gift."

Her mouth fell open in shock. "You don't truly believe that Taylor and Austin did this? They wouldn't do that. That's crazy."

"I don't think they did," he chuckled. "I just wanted to point out that we can't be so quick to rule people out. They had a window of opportunity, plus Taylor spends a lot of time with you. She would have had a chance to possibly make a copy of your house key. She would have known you didn't have any security cameras too."

"Taylor didn't do this."

Shaw was positive of that.

"Once again, I'm not saying that she did. I'm just saying that we have to look at everyone. Even your creepy neighbor across the street, and yes, your ex-boyfriend Eric who apparently can't take no for an answer."

Heat rose in her cheeks. "How did you know about Eric? Melissa?"

"Of course. She suggested that I look into him, and I'm definitely going to do that. If there's anyone else that you've dated in the last year, we should look at them too. Or anyone that asked you out and you turned down."

There was no one else. She didn't have the most active social life with the opposite sex. She'd spent most of her time working.

"You're assuming that the person who did this is close to me."

"When they were only sending you messages, they could have been anywhere in the world. Now they've made contact. They're circling you, getting closer. At the very least, they've been watching you for awhile because they knew you'd be out tonight. That makes me think it's someone you have contact with on a regular basis. It doesn't mean that you've ever spoken a word to them. You know as well as I do that stalkers can create an elaborate fantasy world in their heads and imagine an intimate relationship where none actually exists. There's a possibility that someone saw you on your channel, became obsessed, traveled here from wherever they were, watched you, and is now making contact. I won't say it couldn't happen because I've seen it happen, but that's not an easy thing to do."

It made sense, although she didn't want to think about someone she knew stalking her. She'd much rather it be some random stranger from across the internet. It made it less…personal.

"So what do we do now?"

"I'd suggest sleep, but you said that's not going to happen. How about we play a game to kill some time until the sun comes up? Then tomorrow I'm going to install security cameras around your house. If someone comes again, we'll see them. I'm also going to check out your ex and anyone else that you have contact with, right down to your dry cleaner."

"I don't remember the last time I dry cleaned my clothes. I'm a wash and wear kind of person."

"Then I'll check out your barista and the guy that delivers your pizza."

It was reassuring that Luke was taking this seriously. He wasn't going to let anything happen to her which made her feel safe. But if someone was determined to get to her, they'd find a way. They'd already found her home.

Shaw wanted this to be all over, but she had a feeling that it had only just begun.

HE HAD HER attention. She couldn't ignore him now. His sweet Shaw would soon be his.

CHAPTER TWELVE

T HE SUN WAS barely over the horizon the next morning when Luke heard a soft knock on his back door located in the kitchen. He was tapping away at his laptop while Shaw slumbered in his bed.

She'd finally fallen asleep at about four in the morning, not able to keep her eyes open anymore after three hot chocolates. She'd settled onto the couch but he'd carried her into the bedroom so she wouldn't wake up with a crick in her neck and back.

It was Ryan at the door. Did this bastard ever sleep?

Apparently not. He'd arrived with three hot coffees and a box of pastries.

"I'm worried about you. You're always awake," Luke said as he stepped back to let his friend inside. It was a rainy and chilly day, the sun hiding behind the clouds.

"I told you. I have insomnia. I would have been over earlier, but I assumed you were asleep."

Luke placed his finger over his lips in warning. "I couldn't sleep but Shaw finally dozed off a few hours ago, so let's keep it down. She was exhausted and she needs the rest."

"No problem. I came to bring you some breakfast and see what you needed me to do."

Luke would love Ryan's help, but the guy had his own assignments. It was bad enough that he was taking time from his regular duties to deal with all of this.

"I know you're busier than hell. I'll handle it. I'm going to check out the ex and also set up some security at her house."

Ryan frowned but it quickly turned into a grin. "I can handle a little extra work. I don't sleep, remember? Besides, Logan wants us to be a close team."

"He was at Shaw's last night when the cops were there," Luke conceded. "He did seem like it was okay for me to spend time on this, but I had no idea that he'd ask you to help."

Ryan shrugged. "That's Logan for you. He's an enigma, but he knows what it's like to be stalked…and when it comes to females, he's extra protective. I think he figures that with two of us working on this it will close the case that much faster and then we can get back to our jobs."

"That sounds like something Jared would say."

"Or Reed. Logan also said that the police don't want us sticking our noses into this investigation, so they'll be absolutely no cooperation with them. That's going to be awkward."

It was but Luke had thought about that.

"I'm not planning for them to know that we're looking into anything. If they're not doing it, I doubt they'll notice that we are."

"Interesting perspective but probably true. So what's our plan of attack?"

"I want to set up a security system at Shaw's house. Cameras. An alarm. No one gets in without us knowing."

Ryan's brows shot up. "She's going to go back there? Brave woman."

"I don't want her to," Luke declared firmly. "I'd like it if she stayed here with me, but I have a feeling she's going to insist that she's fine being alone. She's independent as hell. Even if she does stay here, we still need to keep an eye out on the house. He or she might come back."

"What's your gut telling you?" Ryan asked, reaching for a second donut. "Man or woman?"

"My gut isn't talking. The messages haven't been overly romantic so at this point it's a toss-up. Statistically, the majority of stalkers are men, so I've been saying *he*."

Ryan leaned forward, his elbows resting on the table. "If you want to talk about statistics let's start there. The general profile for a stalker is a male, unemployed or underemployed in his thirties to forties with a higher IQ than your general criminal. The majority of victims know their stalker as well."

"Shaw is a public personality, though. That means someone could have seen her channel and fixated on her."

Rubbing his chin, Ryan took another sip of his coffee. "If they've traveled to get close to her, the escalation is through the roof. To go to that much trouble points to some serious delusion. Are you still thinking about her neighbor across the street?"

"He had opportunity. His lights were off last night when I took her home. He might have been out of course, but he could have been sitting in his house watching. He knows that I know what he's doing now so he might be more careful. I'd love to catch that son of a bitch on her property."

"As far as I could find he doesn't have any record of stalking in his past. He doesn't sound like a guy I'd want to have a beer with but that doesn't make him an asshole."

"Because you have high standards."

"Damn right. So we're going to turn your girlfriend's house into Fort Knox. What else do we need to do?"

"Check out her ex-boyfriend. Melissa said his name is Eric Bishop. He was clingy and possessive when they were dating, and Shaw dumped him after a couple of months. He's tried to establish contact several times since then. I want to know what he was doing last night. I also want to have her take me through a typical day. See who she comes in contact with. She's not looking at everyone around her as a potential stalker, but I will."

Ryan nodded in agreement. "Have you thought about taking her away from here for a few days? Get her out of here and de-stress a little? Her birthday went to shit so you could frame it as a late birthday present. A change of scenery might help her."

That wasn't a bad idea. Being less available to her stalker wouldn't be a bad thing.

"I like the idea but where would I take her?"

"There's always something happening in Vegas." Ryan

cleared his throat and tugged at his collar. "My family has a place there. You could stay, free of charge."

Luke had suspicions about his coworker but he'd never put voice to them. Ryan was hiding a couple of things, but he hadn't wanted to pry. When his friend was ready to talk, Luke would be ready to listen.

"I might take you up on that offer."

"I hope you do. Now finish your coffee and let's get started. This admirer isn't going to turn himself in."

With a little luck, he might slip up though, and they'd find him.

Before he got anywhere near Shaw.

SHAW DIDN'T WANT to admit that Luke was making sense. They'd been discussing – intensely – the topic since he'd come back from a trip to the hardware store. They clearly didn't see eye to eye.

"I can't continue to stay with you. I have to stay here. In my home."

She didn't want anyone to run her out of her own house. No one should have that much control over her life.

"That's why I'm placing these cameras here and putting in an alarm system. Although I have to say, Shaw, that I don't think you should be alone. You should stay with me and the dogs where I know you'll be safe."

"If what you say is true, and they've been watching me,

they'll know that I'm at your place."

Luke chuckled and grinned. "They'd be a fool to break into my home. Dylan and Murphy might look lazy and playful, but they'd rip an intruder apart."

Really? The dogs didn't look scary at all. They were large balls of fluff mostly.

Okay, fluff with big teeth.

"How would they know whether it's an intruder?"

"They're sensitive to reactions, especially Dylan." He began opening the myriad of boxes he'd carried into the house. "If you're determined to stay here then you're going to need to beef up your security a great deal. I'm going to put cameras around the house and install an alarm system so that if any doors or windows are breached, you'll be notified. Even if you're not home. You can run the entire system from your phone."

"That sounds high tech. Can someone hack it?"

"Yes, although it would take a tech pro. A general criminal isn't going to know how to do that. I did think about it though, so I purchased cameras that can be hidden. It won't be obvious that you have surveillance."

Surveillance. That's what her life had come to.

"I hate that I need this."

His expression softened and he bent down to drop a kiss on her nose. "I know, honey, and I wish you didn't need this too. Let's just hope that the cameras catch someone lurking around and we can put an end to all of this sooner rather than later."

She could only hope. The stress was wearing on her nerves.

She'd finally nodded off last night, but it had been anything but restful. Her dreams were more like nightmares as she ran from some shadowy figure that hid behind every corner. She'd woken up just as tired as before she'd fallen asleep.

"Is that your plan? Catch him in the act?"

"That would be ideal." He nodded toward her laptop. "Have you checked your messages yet?"

She hadn't. She'd been avoiding it. This was the third time Luke had mentioned it since she'd woken up. He was very sweetly trying not to be pushy but… It had to be done.

"No, because I'm a great big chicken."

"You need to," he said softly. "If he did this, I'm betting he'll tell us himself."

She couldn't delay any longer. He'd already been more than patient. If her "fan" took credit for the incident, then they'd have more information for the police. When she'd checked her laptop last night while they were there, she hadn't received any new messages. Holding her breath, she lifted the lid on her laptop and opened her channel messages, clicking through them and perusing the contents.

There it was. Just one, which these days was unusual. He had sent several the day before but then it was still early. He might send more later.

"There's one here."

Luke rounded the countertop and came to stand next to her, reading over her shoulder. The message was long with quite a bit of angry ranting. He'd come into her home to get her attention since she wouldn't talk to him. He once again warned that if she didn't reply it was only going to get worse. He kept saying that he didn't want to hurt anyone but if he did it would be her fault.

"My fault," she murmured, the words running over and over in her head. "It would all be my fault."

"Don't buy that shit. He's trying to manipulate you. If anyone gets hurt, it's because of the decisions he's made. Not you. He doesn't want to take responsibility for his actions. Tough. The legal system doesn't care about his fucking excuses."

That was true. He might or might not be mentally competent. He appeared to know that what he was doing – or going to do – was wrong but if he had poor impulse control, knowing it wouldn't be enough.

"You're thinking about replying to him, aren't you? It won't help, Shaw. It will only make things much worse."

"I know. He's a bottomless pit of need but I can't help wanting to. I wish that if I replied and gave him some attention this would all go away." She sighed and slumped in the chair. "He'd escalate even more though if I did. It feels like it's all a waste. I keep saving these messages, but for what? You say that you can't trace where they're coming from."

"Changing an IP address is easy. I doubt he'd be stupid enough to use the same address for every profile he's created. Of course, I'll check but I don't think that's going to be our magic bullet."

"What will be our magic bullet?"

Luke smiled and held up one of the cameras he was installing. "Good old-fashioned police work. Observation. Interviews. And a bit of technology. This guy has gotten away with it because you were trying to ignore it. Now we're going to put this front and center. We're going to turn the tables and start going after him, while at the same time he's coming closer. We'll get him."

"You sound so sure."

She wanted to believe him more than anything.

"I am sure. In the meantime, we'll make sure you're safe. He's not going to get near you. I promise."

Shaw had a feeling that Luke was a man who kept his promises.

She was counting on that.

CHAPTER THIRTEEN

LUKE AND RYAN were installing the second to the last camera when a Lexus rolled up into the driveway. An older well-dressed couple exited the vehicle, chatting between themselves, although he couldn't hear exactly what was being said.

Shit and tarnation.

They had to be Shaw's mother and stepfather. He remembered now that she'd mentioned spending the day with her mother last night, but with everything that had gone on since that conversation he'd forgotten about it. Shaw must have as well.

From what she'd said about her mom guilting her all the time this probably wasn't going to go well. As she'd come closer, the older woman appeared agitated and worried, her hands flying around as she spoke in a high-pitched tone.

"I think that's Shaw's parents," Luke said to Ryan. "This might get ugly. You may want to get a snack in the kitchen and hide."

His friend's brows rose and a smile played on his mouth. "Familial strife? I know all about that shit. Maybe I'll go check the motion sensors in the back yard."

"Wise choice."

Ryan disappeared around the corner of the house just as the couple climbed the few front porch steps. Luke was immediately struck by the resemblance between Shaw and her mother. They were both petite and delicate with pale blonde hair, although the older woman's complexion was golden tan as if she spent a great deal of time outdoors. Shaw was far more fair, close to porcelain with a peach-pink tinge to her cheeks.

Jesus, I have it bad for this woman. I'll probably be writing poetry soon.

"Who are you?" the older woman asked bluntly, looking up at him standing on the ladder.

Climbing down, Luke gave them his best and most charming welcoming smile, determined to make a good first impression. This was Shaw's parents, after all.

"Hello, I'm Luke Brewster. I'm a friend of Shaw's. How are you today?"

"Confused," the woman snapped, her lips pressed together tightly. "I was supposed to meet my daughter an hour ago for brunch, but she never showed. Is she here? I can see her car in the garage."

The garage door was up because he and Ryan had been going in and out and using it as a staging area for their work.

"We were supposed to meet her," the older man echoed, although he didn't look near as upset as his wife. "Is she here?"

Luke was about to answer when the front door flew open

and Shaw stood there with what could only be described as a horrified expression.

Yep, she'd forgotten and had just remembered.

"Mom, I'm so sorry! I forgot about our brunch today."

The anguish in Shaw's tone was easy to hear. One look at his new girlfriend and Luke would have known she felt terrible about it. Her mother, however, wasn't looking at her daughter. She was looking at her husband.

"Did you hear that, Oliver? My only daughter forgot all about me. First, she spends her birthday without me and then she simply forgets me. Soon I'll be just a distant memory, I suppose. Next thing you know she'll be spending holidays with strangers instead of her family."

Bingo. Luke now completely understood what Shaw had been describing. If he'd thought she'd exaggerated – and he didn't – he would have been set straight this morning.

"Mom, I'm sorry," Shaw groaned, stepping out onto the front porch. "It wasn't on purpose. There's been a lot going on here last night and this morning."

Her mother feigned relief, her hand fluttering up to her throat. "Oh, thank goodness then. There's a lot going on. That makes me feel so much better. I was just one thing to forget when other issues took your attention. I feel so special now."

Luke almost opened his mouth to tell her that she was making all of this about her but then he thought that perhaps he should keep quiet. Shaw hadn't asked for his help and they had their own family dynamic. They hadn't dated long enough for him to know what she'd want him to do at a moment like this.

So I'll zip it. For now.

Burying her head in her hands, Shaw expelled a noisy breath before lifting her head up again and looking her mother in the eye.

"It wasn't on purpose, Mother." She sighed again and Luke could see that she was fighting an inner battle. Ah, she didn't want to tell her mother what had happened but if she didn't tell her, then her mother would think that Shaw was a bad daughter. A nasty catch-twenty-two. "To be honest, someone broke into my house last night."

Her mother clutched at her chest and then grabbed onto her husband for support. Luke stepped forward in case the woman collapsed but she seemed to steady herself fairly quickly.

"My god, you were robbed? Someone was in your home? I told you living alone wasn't safe, Shaw. I told you that you should move in with us. How else can you be safe?"

Luke could think of a myriad of ways. In fact, he was installing them.

"I am not moving home, Mom. We've talked about this."

"Look what's happened. You're not safe in this neighborhood." The woman's gaze ran contemptuously over the serene and upscale row of homes. "You need to move home immediately. I'll help you pack."

"I'm not moving."

Shaw's voice had gone up, her frustration and irritation showing.

Her mother nudged her husband. "Oliver, tell her she needs to come home with us."

Luke wasn't sure why she thought Shaw's stepfather could convince her. From what she'd described they weren't particularly close or friendly. They barely knew each other.

"Your mother is right, Shaw," Oliver said with an affable smile. "You need to move home. We can take care of you there."

Luke was amused that the three of them had seemingly forgotten he was standing there, a witness to this drama. Even Shaw hadn't given him a glance, her focus honed in on the two people standing across from her on the front porch.

Time to take this inside. She didn't need her neighbors to witness a family brawl.

"How about we all step inside? Have a coffee or some iced tea?" Luke suggested, moving the ladder out of the way. "What do you think, Shaw? Good idea?"

"Yes, let's do that," Shaw replied in the affirmative while shaking her head no. Clearly, she was conflicted about this.

With Ryan hiding in the backyard, Luke and Shaw ushered her parents inside. The three of them settled in the living room but he wasn't sure he should sit down as well. This was her family and her issue. He could be there to help explain the security measures they were taking but dealing with their pressure to move home?

This wasn't his battle to fight.

He didn't want to abandon her either, though. He wanted to be there for support but not be in the way. So he decided to make coffee in the kitchen. Shaw's house wasn't huge so he'd only be a few feet away, he could hear what they were saying, but he wasn't standing in the middle of it all.

"I can make some coffee," he announced. "Shaw, would you like me to do that?"

She gave him a grateful look that he took for a yes. Backing into the kitchen, he began to fill the carafe with water.

"Who is that young man?" her mother asked. "Why is he here? He's certainly making himself at home. Is he living here with you?"

The mother's scandalized tone only served to ratchet up the tension. Luke wasn't even in the living room and he could feel the waves of frustration and animosity in the air.

"Luke is a friend and he's just trying to help. He doesn't live with me."

"It doesn't matter. You need to come back home. It's not safe here."

"It isn't safe anywhere," Shaw argued. "The world isn't an oasis of personal safety, but people go outside and take their chances every day. I'm thirty years old–"

"I know. I didn't get to spend your birthday with you."

"Mother, can we focus on one of your complaints at a time?" Shaw took a breath before continuing. "As I said, I'm thirty years old. I am not going to sell my house and move home with my mother. It's not going to happen. You need to drop this crazy idea."

Uh-oh. She'd called the idea *crazy*. Luke didn't think that was going to go over well.

"Crazy?" Her mother's shrill tone hurt his ears. "It's crazy to want to protect my daughter? My own flesh and blood. I can't believe how ungrateful you've grown up to be after all I've done for you, sacrificed for you. I always put you first, Shaw, before my own happiness and health, and this is how you repay me. It's such a betrayal. My heart is in a million pieces."

Wow, Shaw's mother knew how to play the guilt game. No wonder any boundaries Shaw put into place were completely knocked down time and again.

It only took a few moments for Luke to find three mugs and a tray. The drip coffeemaker was almost done and soon he'd have no other excuse to stay in the kitchen.

"I'm not trying to hurt you, Mother. I'm trying to explain to you that I'm an adult and I'm going to solve my own problems."

"How can you do that? Oliver, tell her that she can't stay here."

That poor bastard Oliver. Shaw's stepfather seemed harmless, but he kept getting shoved in the middle of these arguments. Luke had to wonder if this happened often. Probably it did.

"I think you should listen to your mother, Shaw," Oliver piped up. "She knows best."

It was like being in some weird television show where reality wasn't a thing. Luke's parents would rightly be worried about him if he had a stalker or someone had broken into his home but there was no way they'd pressure him to move back.

Was it different because he was male? Would his parents do this to Melissa or one of his other sisters? He didn't think so, but he might be wrong.

Carrying the tray of coffee cups out to the living room, Luke set it on the table in between three people.

"Here's your coffee," he said, a bit louder than he needed to. "I'm just going to go back into the kitchen and then check on Ryan in the back yard. See if he needs any help."

He slipped back into the kitchen and then out of the back door where Ryan was sitting on a lawn chair and fiddling with his phone.

"Did you hear any of that?"

Looking up, Ryan shook his head. "The windows are closed and I'm not a wolf. Is it bad?"

"It isn't good. I feel badly for Shaw. She's getting the shit end of the stick in there."

Grinning, Ryan stood up and stretched. "And you want to go in there and save her. Right?"

"I do," Luke confessed. "But I think she'd take off my arm if I did. She's definitely not into that damsel in distress stuff."

"It's best to stay out of family disputes," Ryan replied. "You two haven't been seeing each other that long either. Discretion is the way to go here."

"Is that what you'd do?"

"Absolutely…probably. Unless it got violent or something. Then I'd intervene for sure."

Luke didn't think it was going to get that bad in there. It was bad enough, though. Shaw didn't need these extra problems at a time like this.

With parents like that, a stalker might not be her biggest issue.

CHAPTER FOURTEEN

SHAW WAS AT her wit's end. She'd had a shitty birthday, a restless night, and now she was operating on too little sleep, not enough, caffeine, and the fear that she couldn't shake. To add to her misery, Julia was being a pain in the ass. More so than usual. Her mother had always had a flair for the dramatic but even Shaw hadn't predicted that it would be this bad.

"You aren't safe here," Julia insisted. "You can't live by yourself."

I definitely can't live with you.

Taking a steadying breath, Shaw tried to talk her mother down from the ledge she'd hopped up on.

"Luke and his friend are setting up a secure alarm system with cameras around the house. Rock stars don't have this much security. I'll be fine."

Hopping up from her spot on the couch, Julia paced the small area in front of the picture window.

"I can't believe how foolhardy you're being. You could be killed."

"I could be killed in a car accident. We all take chances every day. I'm actually taking far less chances now that the security system is installed. I'll one able to monitor every corner of my property from my phone."

"From your phone?" Oliver asked, his brows shooting up. "How do you do that?"

"It's easy. I'll show you." Retrieving her phone, Shaw opened the app that Luke had installed for her. He'd shown her how to switch from camera to camera and there was even a panic button to call the police. "See? I can see Luke and Ryan in the back yard, plus see all around the house and partially down the street."

Her stepfather studied the screen and then handed it to Julia. "You have to admit, honey, that this is impressive."

"They also installed motion sensors outside, and on the windows and doors. If anyone walks into the yard, the floodlights go on. If anyone tries to open a door or window, the alarm will sound and automatically call the police."

Julia dumped the phone on the end table. "If someone wants into your house, they'll find a way. Right, Oliver? Tell her that this isn't foolproof."

"Your mother is right about that, Shaw. Where there's a will there's a way."

Luke had already explained the shortcomings in the system. A determined hacker could get into it and there were jammers sold that could turn off the cameras, but it was better than having nothing. They were going to continue down the path that her stalker wasn't a professional criminal and wouldn't have a working knowledge of remote cameras and alarms.

"It's a deterrent," Shaw insisted. "Robbers want easy targets."

She didn't want to tell them that this break-in wasn't about stealing her laptop. This was about so much more. If Julia found out, she'd probably faint dead away on Shaw's maple flooring.

"I can see you're not going to listen to sense," Julia replied, sweeping her arm toward the back door. "That new man in your life has filled your head with nonsense. It wouldn't surprise me if he was the one that broke into your house last night."

"He couldn't have. He was with me."

Oops. She hadn't intended to mention that either. It only served to make Julia even more enraged, her face a bright red.

"Were you even going to tell me you had a new boyfriend? I guess I know where I stand." Julia whirled around on her high heel and grabbed her purse and coat. "Oliver, let's go. I've been hurt about as much as I can stand by my only child. I need to lie down."

Julia was known for taking to her bed when life wasn't cooperating. Now Shaw was responsible for the latest episode.

Awesome. This is just great. I'm a terrible child.

Oliver gave Shaw a reproachful look as he gathered his own coat and they marched out of the front door. Shaw followed, feeling absolutely miserable about...well...everything. She didn't want to hurt anyone, least of all her own mother. But if she told Julia the truth the shit would truly hit the fan.

"I'm sorry, Mom," she heard herself saying. "I wish you could understand where I'm coming from here."

Julia paused at the bottom porch step. "I don't think we

should talk about this right now. I'm going home."

It wasn't over though. Shaw was sure that her mother would be back with more arguments and more tears. This was only the opening salvo in an ongoing war.

Her parents had zoomed out of the driveway so Shaw went back into the house, falling back on the couch cushions with a huge sigh. She should never have brought up that someone broke into her house. She should have taken the hit that she'd simply forgotten lunch. Julia would have lost her mind and been angry but then it would eventually be over. This was going to go on forever.

"Is the coast clear?"

She'd briefly forgotten all about Luke in the back yard. Dammit, he'd seen all her dirty laundry when it came to her family. He'd see that while she could give advice she sure as hell couldn't take it.

"It is," she confirmed. "You were smart to clear the premises. I would have if I could."

"Were you disowned?"

"I wish." She levered off the couch and came to stand by him. She needed a hug or something, but she didn't know how to ask for it. "She's taking to her bed which is far worse. I'll be blamed for that, of course, and anything else that happens for the next week or so."

"I didn't hear anything after I went outside but I can see that you have a few issues with your mom. You're right about her knowing exactly how to guilt you for maximum pressure."

"I feel like shit," Shaw said bluntly. "Like absolute and utter shit."

Luke cocked his head. "Because you didn't cave and put the house up for sale?"

"Because I…"

She didn't know what to say.

"Because I made her upset."

"You're upset too," Luke reminded her gently. He reached out and slowly pulled her into his arms, letting her move away if she wanted to. She didn't want to. This was heaven, being held like she really mattered. "The last twenty or so hours for you have been hell. Don't you get to be emotional about that too?"

"She doesn't know all of the facts. I didn't want to tell her about the stalker. She would have been even worse if I had. She would have packed my bags personally and dragged me bodily to the car."

"Honey, think about what you've just said to me. You're saying that your mother would have treated her grown daughter like a child. Is that okay with you? You've made a decision to stay here. I don't agree with it because I think you should stay with me or Melissa until we catch this guy, but I respect that decision because you are an adult. I don't have to like everything that you do. She doesn't either, but she needs to understand that you're grown up. She doesn't get to make the rules anymore."

"Tell her that," Shaw muttered, resting her cheek against Luke's broad chest. She could hear the strong and steady thump of his heart under her ear and feel the warmth from his skin through his clothes. For the first time today, she felt…safe and protected. Was she being stubborn saying that she was going to stay in her own home? Was she being foolish as her mother had said? "You should have seen the fit she threw when I bought this place. She took to her bed for a week that time."

Julia had given Shaw the silent treatment for almost a month too.

"She's trying to control you, and you know it. You can't change your mother, but you can change how you respond."

"I know that, it's just…"

"It's your mother," he guessed. "There's a bunch of emotional baggage between a parent and a child and she's had years to install the guilt chip."

"It's deeply embedded into my psyche," she agreed. "I know that she's doing this to try and control me. I know that our relationship is dysfunctional. But when I try to change, she goes ballistic and then we fall back into our old ways."

"You know what you have to do. If there's any way I can help, let me know. I'm here for you."

She cuddled against him more closely. "Yes, you are."

Chuckling, he dropped a kiss on the top of her head. "Do you think we should let Ryan back into the house?"

Groaning, she slapped her forehead. "He must think I'm an idiot. Of course, he can come back in."

"He doesn't think you're an idiot. He's made mention of his family once or twice. I think he has about the same relationship with them that you have with your mom."

"Then I feel sorry for him. I'll go out and apologize and then maybe we can order a pizza. Are you hungry?"

Stepping back, Luke spread his arms out wide. "Look at me. I'm always hungry."

Pizza wouldn't make all of this go away, but it might make her feel a little better.

"You know, Ryan made a suggestion this morning that I think might be a good idea. How about you and I take off for a few days? Just you and me. Get out of town and see some new sights. We can try and celebrate your birthday a second time."

"I don't want this guy to chase me away."

"It's not running away, you're running to something. Specifically, Vegas. Just think about it. We could get on the next flight. I'll talk to my boss."

It was on the tip of her tongue to say that if she left after her argument with Julia it would upset her mother even more.

I can't worry about how she'll react when I make perfectly normal adult decisions.

Shaw had to insert her spine and make some changes with her mother or they were going to be caught in this never-ending cycle until one of them died.

And the way her luck was going lately with a stalker and all, it just might be her first.

"I'll think about Vegas."

LUKE DIDN'T WANT to leave Shaw but she was determined that

she wasn't going to be run out of her own home. He'd left Ryan there to finish the motion sensors and he'd told Shaw that if she changed her mind he'd be there as quickly as possible. No questions asked. No saying *I told you so.*

He had a suspicion that when the sun went down staying in that house all alone was going to look a hell of a lot different than it had when it was shiny and bright outside. It was easy to have bravado at two in the afternoon.

"Jared did some digging for you on that guy Eric Bishop."

Luke had traveled to Logan's home because he'd received a text that there was information about Shaw's clingy ex-boyfriend.

"Where's Ryan?" Logan asked as they sat down in the kitchen. His wife Ava had left them a pitcher of iced tea and a plate of cookies. She'd left with the twins to see a movie. "I thought he was helping you with this."

"He's finishing up the security system install so I could come here."

Logan nodded absently. "Good. Glad you're getting that done. How's your girl doing?"

"She's brave. She's determined to stay in her house tonight."

That statement made Logan look up from the file folder and grin. "She sounds a lot like Ava then. I take it you're not happy about this decision."

"I don't think it's the best idea. I'm planning to camp out on her street and watch the house from my car tonight."

Throwing back his head, Logan laughed. "I can see that

you're as stubborn as she is. Can you stay awake all night?"

"With a little help from some strong coffee I should be okay. I'll grab a nap when I leave here and then head back to her place. I've been on some damn boring stakeouts in my time. I want to keep an eye out on that neighbor James Hornsby. He's creepy as shit watching her all the time."

"You might change your mind when I tell you what Jared's found. Turns out Eric Bishop has a history of not being able to take no for an answer. It was with the campus police where he went to college, so it wasn't easy to find but when we did there was more than a few females who had lodged complaints about him. He'd follow, call, send gifts. The usual. I think he might be your best bet."

"I might have to pay him a visit."

Logan handed over a slip of paper. "Here's his address. How are you going to handle this? You're not on a case. You can't go in there officially. The local police don't want you anywhere near their investigation."

"They don't have an investigation," Luke pointed out. "They think Shaw is blowing this out of proportion."

"Did you let them know about the email from her fan taking credit for the birthday cake?"

"She did. They gave her the same advice her agent gave her. Block the guy. Get a security system. Let them know immediately if he shows up. They said they would update the police report to reflect the new information. Basically, they can't do much until we find the guy, then she can file a restraining order."

"The current laws are set up so that she kind of has to know who is harassing her before the police can do much. Her channel provider doesn't sound like they're doing much either."

"They've blocked his IP address but he just uses a new one. It's like playing whack-a-mole. I doubt he's even using his own Wi-Fi. I'd guess he's going to the library or coffee shops."

"You'll find him. I have confidence in you."

Luke scratched his chin. "Listen, about that. I know I'm spending a lot of time–"

"It's okay." Logan waved off his apology. "Your cases have been temporarily reassigned. We can spare you for a little while. Now if this stretches out, we'll need to have a talk about what we need to do."

"I don't want this to jeopardize my chances of being chosen for the permanent team." Luke took a deep breath. "In fact, I was thinking that I might take Shaw out of town for a few days. Decompress from all of this stress. I was going to talk to you about it."

"It won't jeopardize anything." Logan picked up a chocolate chip cookie and bit into it. "And you can take a few days if you need to. I know you, Brewster, and you'll continue to work even if you're not in the office. I'll be honest with you. Jared, Jason, Reed, and I talked this through, and we've decided to let you work on this because it's a much better audition of your skills than any cold case. This is the real fucking deal so don't blow it."

Shit. Just...shit. They were evaluating his performance on *this.*

Logan grinned and clapped Luke on the shoulder. "Now don't let that intimidate you. We're sure you can handle this."

No pressure. He only had to worry about keeping Shaw safe and making the elite serials and stalkers task force. Piece of cake, really. No big deal.

I'd better get to work.

CHAPTER FIFTEEN

LUKE HAD LEFT to go to a meeting with his boss, but his friend Ryan had stayed behind to complete the installation of Shaw's shiny new security system. It was slick as could be, allowing her to see her house whether she was inside of it or in another state completely. It did help to make her feel more secure, knowing that any movement outside would set off the floodlights. The sensors on the doors and windows were an added bonus too. Luke had joked that she now lived in Fort Knox.

Retrieving a bottle of water from the refrigerator, she opened the back door to offer Ryan some water but he was standing right there, his hand outstretched as if to turn the doorknob.

"I didn't scare you, did I?" he asked, a wide smile on his face. "I was coming in to let you know that I'm all done out here."

She held up the water. "I was coming to offer you a cool drink."

"I'll take it, thanks."

Stepping back to allow him inside, Shaw handed over the bottle.

"So you work with Luke?"

She wasn't sly and Ryan knew exactly what she was trying to do if the twinkle in his eye was to be believed.

"I do. What do you want to know, Shaw?"

Heat flooded her cheeks, but she'd gone this far already so she might as well just go all the way.

"He seems like a really nice guy."

"He *is* a really nice guy. One of the best. I haven't known him all that long, just since we started working together earlier this year, but I can see that he's a good person. He'd give you the shirt off of his back and never remind you of it again. He's a loyal friend."

Great, now Shaw had a vision of Luke walking around without his shirt. The heat in her cheeks was only the tip of the iceberg. Luke had an amazing physique. Not that she wouldn't like him if he didn't…but he did.

"I guess I just wondered if he's all that he seems to be."

"He is. His whole family is that way. I met them all on the Fourth of July. His parents had a cookout. They're close to one another. You could see the bond that they have. Not that I've ever personally experienced it, but they made me feel like part of the family the minute they met me."

Her ears perked up at his casual statement. "You have family issues too?"

Smirking, Ryan took a drink from the water bottle. "My issues have issues. Let's just say that I'm the family black sheep."

"The black sheep? How so?"

Leaning a hip against the kitchen counter, Ryan rubbed at his chin. "Can I trust you with a secret? Not even Luke knows. My bosses do, of course, because I swear they know everything, but no one else does."

Could she keep a secret? Yes, she could. Even from Luke. Because all her friends from high school on had come to her with their problems and asking for advice, she'd become something of an expert in keeping secrets.

"I can. I promise I won't tell anyone."

"You see...it's like this. My family is rich. As in filthy rich. Old money too, the kind that sticks around for generations and isn't talked about because it would be tacky."

It was the last thing that Shaw had expected Ryan to say.

"You come from money?"

"Yes."

"I'm not sure how that plays into not experiencing family harmony."

"Sorry, I sometimes assume that people get what I'm saying without me spelling it out. My family has a long tradition of business and finance. Guess who didn't join the family business? That would be me. I'm a huge disappointment to my father and grandfather. I wouldn't marry the daughter of another rich family to join the dynasties, either. That was a huge sin on my part."

"Do people really do that? I thought that was just in books and movies."

Ryan nodded grimly. "They do, although they pretend it's

for love. I wouldn't play ball and they're still pissed about it. My father and mother still wonder how they failed as parents when it came to me. I haven't done anything that they wanted me to do."

"They didn't want you to be a cop?"

"My family believes that we buy cops. And attorneys, and politicians. You get the idea. Getting my hands dirty with actual dirt? Not a good look for a Beck."

"What did they want you to be?"

"A senator and eventually the president of the United States."

Uh, wow. The family was certainly ambitious. Shoot for the stars and all of that.

"And you wanted to be a cop?"

He nodded, a smile playing on his lips. "I was downtown with my old man and there was a bank robbery on the same street. I saw how the police handled it and from that moment on I knew what I wanted to be when I grew up. It was my sole focus."

"So they're mad at you?"

"Yes, and whenever I see them, which isn't often, they remind me of what a disappointment I am. They also tell me that they still hold out hope that I'll repent and come back into the family fold. Fat chance of that happening."

"So they try to control you?"

There were parallels here to her own situation.

"Sure, and for a long time I let them guilt me into doing shit that I didn't want to do. A prep school education, a fancy university. Country clubs, golf, elegant dinner parties, and the rest of that crap. They couldn't control me with money after I turned twenty-one, so they used guilt. Damn, they were good at it too. But eventually, it didn't work anymore."

She needed to know why.

"How did it stop working?"

He shrugged carelessly. "They kept using the same old tired lines and tricks. It became repetitive and eventually it wasn't effective anymore. I'm guessing that your parents also use the guilt card with you?"

"She invented the guilt card. She's a master at pushing all my buttons. Every single one."

"Then don't let her."

"That's easier said than done," Shaw groaned. "What's your secret?"

"Do you really want to know? You aren't going to like the answer."

She wanted to know. She *needed* to know.

"I truly do want to know. I'm losing my mind here and I can't keep doing this."

"Okay, I'll tell you." He leaned down and his voice dropped to a whisper. "If you want to stop feeling guilty then you have to not care what she thinks."

"I don't care what she thinks."

His smile was one of disbelief. "I don't think so. I think you're where I was a few years ago. I kept thinking that if I just stayed true to my beliefs and became a success on my own terms that eventually my parents would respect my independence and approve of my life. Spoiler alert. That was a huge nope. They aren't going to change, and the chances are that your mom isn't going to change either. She might, but you can't bank on that. You have to get to the point where you don't need their approval anymore. You have to not care. Because the only way that my parents were going to approve my life was if I lived it their way. Full stop. Their approval was too expensive, Shaw. It cost me way too much of my soul. How much will it cost you?"

Far too much.

"You don't think that they'll ever be proud of you?"

He shook his head. "They want an unconditional surrender. I can't do that. Not even for my mother and father. I love them but I'm not going to live my life for them. That's asking too much. But you have to decide that for yourself."

"Are they angry with you?"

"Sure, sometimes. Last Christmas, my mom threw a little tantrum and my dad gave me the usual speech of how I'd *made* my mother upset. The thing is...I don't think that I did. The way she acted you'd have thought I told them I was joining a traveling carnival. I just told them I was taking this new job. That's it. My mom *decided* to get upset. I told my dad that I wasn't that powerful. I couldn't make anyone upset. He was trying to shift responsibility for my mother's emotions to me, but she's a grown woman. She has to be responsible."

How many times had Julia done that to Shaw? Made her

daughter responsible for her emotions and reactions? Even when she was just a child? Too many to count.

"I think that maybe you and I grew up with the same sort of parents."

"My mom and dad are nice people, but they think they should get their way all the time. I think that perhaps I'm the universe's way of reminding them that they don't run the world. Although they'd love to do that."

"You've given me a lot to think about," Shaw finally said after a long silence. "Breaking a pattern of behavior that I've fallen back on for years isn't going to be easy."

"It's work," Ryan agreed, emptying the water bottle. "And it's going to be hell. Mark my words. They won't give in quietly. You'll have to stick to your guns time and time again."

"Does it still bother you? Just a little?"

His gaze dropped to the floor and then flickered back up to Shaw. "I think the hardest part is that like all people I want to be loved for myself. I want them to love me for who and what I am. But here's the most important thing...I've found that the opinions of people who were important to me in my youth simply don't hold the weight that they used to as I've become an adult. I think that's the way it's supposed to be. I can respect them as my parents and still not worry about their approval."

Could Shaw accept that? Could she finally get to the point where her mother's approval wasn't important?

It was far past time to find out.

★ ★ ★

LUKE HAD GONE over this a million times in his head, each iteration a little different than the one before. He wasn't supposed to be inserting himself into Shaw's investigation, and Logan had warned him not to call any attention to himself. He had to fly under the radar at all times.

So he'd decided to approach Eric Bishop as a person asking for help. No accusations, no good cop and bad cop. Just a request for any information that Bishop might have. Simple and straightforward. Then Luke would watch the guy's reactions and answers extremely carefully, looking for any signs of deceit.

Eric Bishop managed an upscale restaurant in a suburb of Seattle. The kind that was hard to get reservations for and when you did the portions were incredibly small. Not Luke's kind of place, but then he was more of a wings and beer type. He didn't know shit about wine pairings either.

"Is Eric Bishop here this evening?" he asked the young hostess when she asked if he had a reservation. "I was hoping that I could speak briefly with him."

"Um, just a minute." She picked up the phone on her desk and spoke quietly in it for a moment. "He'll be right out."

"Thank you."

Luke stepped aside so that the party behind him could be seated. While waiting he studied the old black and white photos on the wall of Seattle at the turn of the century.

"That one is from 1907," he heard a voice say behind him.

"Amazing to think that this is the same city, isn't it?"

"It is," Luke agreed, turning to greet the other man. "Hi, my name is Luke Brewster. I was hoping to get a few minutes of your time."

They shook hands but Eric Bishop didn't look like he was all that thrilled about having a visitor. Luke couldn't blame him though. He had to be wondering what the hell Luke wanted.

"I'm a friend of Shaw Parker's," Luke explained, watching Bishop's expression closely. "I was hoping you might be able to help me...and her."

Bishop's eyes widened, and he beckoned Luke to follow him down a hallway. "Shaw? Is she okay? Of course, I'll help. Let's just step into my office for privacy."

They walked through a door at the end of the hallway into a small, utilitarian office with a metal desk, a couple of chairs, and a worn loveseat shoved up against the wall. Bishop reached for the desk phone. "Would you like something to drink? I can get one of the waitresses to bring you something."

"No, thank you. I don't want to take up much of your time."

Bishop sat behind his desk and Luke settled into one of the wooden chairs on the other side.

"So how can I help you? I mean, help Shaw? Is she okay? Is she hurt or sick?"

Luke shook his head. "She's fine. But she does have a problem that I'm trying to solve for her. You see, someone has been harassing Shaw online and recently in person. They entered her home on her birthday while she was out. Left her a few things to find. Obviously, she's upset about it and I'm trying to find out who might have done it."

Watching the other man's reaction closely, Luke leaned forward in his chair so they were eye to eye. Bishop was in the power position behind the desk, but Luke didn't want him to get too comfortable. This was a friendly discussion, but the goal was to keep the other man off balance if at all possible.

Bishop's expression first went from confused to concerned and then back to confused. No flicker of guilt or recognition.

"That's terrible but I'm not sure how I can be of help."

"You and Shaw dated for a few months, right? During that time was anyone in her life giving her any sort of inappropriate attention? Maybe the guy that delivers her paper or the person that makes her coffee? Anyone that might have been a little too familiar or persistent?"

Keep it friendly. Gain his trust.

Bishop's eyes widened and he straightened in his chair. "As a matter of fact, yes. Her neighbor across the street. He was always around whenever I was there. We'd be getting out of the car and he'd walk up and just start talking to Shaw as if I wasn't there. I found it very strange, to be honest. I definitely think he had a crush on her."

"Did you say anything to Shaw about him?"

The other man shook his head. "I could tell that she thought it was harmless, and that she didn't have any interest in him. I assumed that he would eventually get the hint, but it sounds like maybe he didn't. Do you think he might have broken into her house?"

"I haven't ruled anyone out at his point."

"Are you a cop?" Bishop asked, squirming slightly in his seat. "I guess I'm confused as to your relationship with Shaw."

That wasn't any of Eric Bishop's business, and Luke didn't want to stoke any emotions just in case this guy was the stalker.

"I'm a friend who used to be a cop," Luke replied. "My sister is a good friend of Shaw's. You may remember her. Her name is Melissa."

Looking relieved, Bishop nodded. "Of course, Melissa. I remember her. She was really nice. It's great that you're helping out. Not many brothers would do that."

"I've always been close to my family, plus I feel badly that Shaw is having to deal with this."

"She's an amazing person," Bishop agreed, his fingers smoothing down his tie. "Wonderful, really. Have you talked to anyone else? I mean, anyone else she dated after me?"

This guy wasn't all that smooth. It was easy to see that the answer mattered to him. A lot.

"I've been talking to pretty much anyone who knows her."

"Right, right. That would make sense."

Sitting back in his chair, Luke gave Bishop a friendly smile. "So have you been in contact with Shaw lately?"

Clearing his throat, Bishop shook his head. "No, I haven't spoken with her in quite awhile."

"But you've texted her."

Luke didn't phrase it as a question, because he knew for a

fact that Eric Bishop had sent a text as recently as two weeks ago.

"Just to ask her how she's doing," Bishop replied defensively. "Shaw and I are still good friends, you see."

They really were not but this wasn't the time to argue the point.

"It's nice that you've stayed friends," Luke said instead, rising from his chair. "I do appreciate your time this evening and thank you for answering a few of my questions."

Bishop also rose from his chair and nervously ran his hand down his silk tie. Again.

"I always want to help a friend. I hope you look more closely at her neighbor. He seemed a little strange."

Placing his hand on the doorknob, Luke paused before exiting the office. "Just one more question, if you don't mind. Where were you the night of the twelfth, Mr. Bishop? Between seven and midnight."

The other mans' lips pressed into a thin line and his eyes narrowed in anger. "I was here. Any of the staff can verify that. Why do you ask?"

"Just good housekeeping. I need to make sure that I rule out everyone so that I can concentrate on the right people."

"I would never hurt Shaw," he said between gritted teeth. "I care about her."

"I appreciate you being so honest. Thank you." Luke opened the door and the sounds of voices drifted into the office. "I should be going now. As I said, thank you so much for talking to me tonight. You've been a great help."

"That's all I want to do. Help Shaw if she needs it."

Luke bid the man goodbye and headed for his car. He needed to get back to Shaw's soon. He didn't like leaving her alone even though she was determined to be that way.

But this trip to see Eric Bishop had been worth it. He was far too attached still for an ex-boyfriend. As for whether his staff would back him up, Luke assumed that they would. It would, however, be fairly easy to sneak out the back door, go to Shaw's house, and then sneak back in. There was an exit right next to Bishop's office.

He was still on Luke's list.

CHAPTER SIXTEEN

AFTER RYAN LEFT, Shaw wandered around the house, checking out the cameras and making sure the doors and windows were locked. She was safe and secure in her home, Luke and his friend had made sure of it, but now that the sun was going down and darkness was creeping in she was beginning to feel increasingly restless.

I chose this. I didn't want to leave.

Those thoughts didn't make anything better though. She kept walking around, peeking out the curtains to the house across the street. The lights were off again. Perhaps James wasn't home. Or if he was, then he had all the lights off which was a creepy thought in and of itself. For a moment, an image of him sitting in the dark – all alone in his living room – flashed through her mind. It was unsettling.

I'm wound way too tight.

A hot bath and glass of wine would do the trick. She filled the tub and then sunk down into it, letting all of her muscles relax and go limp. She took a sip from the wine glass on the edge of the tub and then let her head fall back, her eyes fluttering closed.

Heaven. This feels so good.

Sliding deeper down, Shaw let the water lap around her chin. She needed this. The last twenty-four hours had been far too stressful.

What I need is a week on the beach, listening to the waves.

That wasn't such a bad idea, actually. She could move her schedule around, pre-film several episodes for her channel. She could make it a girls' trip with Melissa and Taylor...or a romantic getaway with just her and Luke. They hadn't done much physically yet, but the undercurrent of desire was there between them. She could feel it and he did too. It was only a matter of time before they threw caution to the wind and ended up naked and sweaty between the sheets.

If Luke was as thorough and caring in bed as he was out... It was going to be good. So very good. She had a feeling that they were going to have great chemistry. Frankly, she'd been disappointed in the past, but she'd never felt this sort of heat with anyone else before.

She *liked* him. A lot. He was smart, funny, and caring. Plus, they had an intense attraction. It was weird that only a few weeks ago she'd been telling her friends that she didn't care if she was in a relationship. She was fine alone. Now she couldn't imagine her life without this man in it. It had happened so quickly, but here she was.

I'm not mad about it either.

Reaching for the wine glass again, she had to sit up to take another sip. Shaw wasn't a big drinker, but she liked a fruity wine on occasion. She'd never be one of those people who tasted a wine and could guess the vintage.

Thump. Thump.

The glass paused halfway to her lips, her hand frozen in midair. What was that?

Shaw stayed perfectly still, straining to hear any sound from the rest of the house.

Thump. Thump.

It wasn't the ice maker in the refrigerator. She knew that sound. It wasn't the heater kicking on either. It wasn't any of the familiar sounds that a home makes and a resident becomes accustomed to. No house was truly silent even when there was only one occupant.

Fuck. I left my phone in the bedroom.

If she'd had it, she could have checked all the cameras but of course she'd placed it on the nightstand. She hadn't wanted to be interrupted while soaking in the tub.

Levering out of the bath, she quickly ran a towel over her wet limbs and then slipped on her robe and slippers. It wasn't the best outfit for investigating suspicious noises, but it was going to have to do.

Treading softly into the bedroom, she immediately opened the security app and scanned through the cameras on the outside of the house. The clarity of the picture was surprisingly good despite the lack of any sun whatsoever. It appeared that the motion-sensor light at the front of the house had been triggered but nowhere else. She didn't see anyone either, not even a squirrel.

Anything could have triggered that light out front. A jogger or a dog.

Ryan had warned her before he left that they would probably have to fine tune the motion sensors. He told her to let them know if birds or passing cars set them off.

That's all it was. A passerby. Probably a car. And the noise could have been a bird or a squirrel. Maybe even a stray cat. I've seen those around the neighborhood. I'm overreacting.

She was letting this situation get into her head and freak her out. Normally, she was as level-headed as they come, but she'd allowed this asshole to make her feel afraid.

That pissed her off. She didn't want some stranger running her life. She was already struggling to be independent from her own mother.

Tucking the phone into the pocket of her robe, she went back into the bathroom to retrieve the wine glass and pour the contents down the sink. Alcohol wasn't the answer tonight. She needed to keep a clear head on her shoulders.

Rinsing the glass in the kitchen sink, she felt the phone in her pocket buzz with a text. Luke perhaps? He'd told her he had some business to take care of in the office, but it would be nice to talk to him. They'd planned to have breakfast together in the morning.

Okay, I miss him already.

The text was from a number she didn't recognize. She

opened it and a video began to play on loop. Her fingers tightened on the phone, the knuckles going white as the breath caught in her chest.

It was the cake and candles from last night.

Grabbing onto the countertop to keep her knees from giving out, a horrified Shaw watched the video over and over, scarcely believing her own eyes. Whoever had been in her house last night had taped themselves putting the cake on the table and lighting the candles. And now they'd sent her the video for her entertainment.

Were they the ones making that noise?

Were they here at her home? Outside? Were they watching?

Her heart in her throat, she frantically pressed buttons to stop the video and pull up her phone contact list, scrolling to Luke. A few more buttons and his phone was ringing.

"Shaw, how–"

"Luke," she cut in, not letting him speak. "I just got a text from an unknown number. It's a video of the person that left the cake and lit the candles last night. I can't see who it is, but they sent it to me."

"Okay, okay," he said in a soothing tone. "I'm going to come right there, okay? We're going to stay on the phone while I do it."

He didn't understand. Mostly because she wasn't making much sense.

"Luke, I was in the bathtub and I heard noises. Thumping noises. So I got out of the bathtub and checked the cameras but I didn't see anything although the front light was triggered. Then my phone buzzed and I–"

"Shaw," Luke said in a firm voice, interrupting her explanation. "Open the front door for me. I'm right outside."

Outside? He couldn't be outside. He was at home or at the office.

"You don't understand," Shaw repeated, desperation and fear making her sound squeaky. "You need–"

"Shaw," Luke said louder this time. "Open the front door. I am standing on the other side. Check the cameras if you don't believe me."

There was no way he could be on the other side, but her shaky fingers fumbled to open the app.

There he was. Standing on her front porch.

Flying to the door, she jerked it open and crashed into him. He was solid and real and exactly what she needed at this moment.

"Easy, honey," Luke said, pulling her into his arms and literally lifting her up and carrying her to the couch, his foot kicking the door closed behind them. "I've got you. I'm here."

Clinging to him like a life preserver, she buried her face in his neck, breathing in his warm scent to help center herself.

"How are you even here? You're supposed to be at the office."

"I was done with work a while ago. I know you said you wanted to be on your own, but I thought you might be nervous. Plus, I frankly don't trust this son of a bitch even with cameras and an alarm system. I was watching you from my car a few houses down."

She'd be angry about that tomorrow. He hadn't trusted her to take care of herself and she should be pissed the hell off, but at the moment why or how he was here didn't matter. It only mattered that he was.

"I'm going to yell at you later."

He nodded, his stubbly chin rubbing against her temple. "I fully expect you to. I was wrong to do it and you should be angry. I'll grovel for forgiveness."

"I am glad you're here."

"I'm glad too." He pushed a strand of hair away from her face. "Can you show me the video?"

"Yes. It's creepy."

They settled on the couch and she showed him the text she'd received from the unknown number. He'd said that he would check it out but spoofing numbers was easy and it would probably just be a dead end.

A dead end. Like everything else. She ought to be used to it by now.

Luke watched it several times, getting more frustrated with each viewing.

"The bastard didn't give us much, did he?" Luke said grimly, handing her back the phone. "The lighting sucks and we didn't see much of his hands either. I'll have to take that video to work and have it enhanced. Maybe we can see an identifying feature."

"If you had an identifying feature, would you allow it to be filmed?"

"No, but he might not be aware of modern technology that would allow us to see things that he didn't count on."

Shaw didn't have much hope. So far, this person hadn't made any mistakes.

"Did you see my front porch light go on?"

"I did. A couple with their dog walked by on the sidewalk. We'll need to fine tune the motion sensor. They actually set off a few others before yours. Looks like more than a few people have installed some security."

Shaw nodded toward the window. "Are the lights still out? I mean, James's lights?"

Luke stood and pulled the curtain back slightly. "I didn't see any lights all evening and it's still dark over there. Have you seen your neighbor at all today?"

"No. He might be traveling again. He does that a lot."

Dropping the curtain, Luke turned back to her. "I think it would be best if you didn't stay here tonight. You won't get any sleep and neither will I, although that was my original plan. Why don't you pack a bag and we can go back to my place? Tomorrow we'll reassess and figure out what to do."

She couldn't wait to leave her house yet at the same time she didn't want to go. She didn't want this asshole to win, running her out of her own home. He shouldn't get to do that, and it made her angry.

"Wow, your whole expression changed in seconds," Luke said. "You went from scared to furious in about two-point-two seconds."

"I am mad," Shaw admitted. "I'm mad that I have to leave my house. I hate that he's winning."

Luke shook his head. "This isn't a battle. At least not yet. He's not winning anything. We're just moving our base of operations temporarily to regroup and get a new plan. As I said before, he's clearly escalating and he's doing it quickly. As for being angry, I think you have a good reason for it, and it's healthy not to sit back passively. Get mad, get all pissed off, and then let's do something to make this situation go away. For good."

"Passivity is not an issue that I think is a problem for me."

"That's the best attitude because action is your friend in a case like this."

"A case like this," she echoed with a sigh. "That sounds so fucking depressing."

"I know but it is what it is. It's better to be clear about what we're dealing with. You have a stalker, Shaw. There is a person stalking you, and they're getting closer. In my experience, that's usually not a good thing. On the other hand, it gives us a chance to catch the asshole which can be a positive."

"I want him caught. I want him – or her – out of my life."

There were many things she wasn't sure of but that one fact she knew to be true. She wanted her life back. It hadn't been perfect, but it had been hers. Now it was beginning to feel like it belonged to someone else. He was calling the shots and she was only reacting.

"We'll get him."

Shaw wanted to believe that with all her heart.

"I'm going to go get dressed and pack a bag."

"I'll call Melissa. She was going to watch Dylan and Murphy for me tonight, but I'll let her know that we're heading back to my place."

Inwardly groaning, Shaw rubbed at her temples. "Poor Melissa, getting dragged into my problems. And poor you. I doubt you signed up for this when she suggested we have coffee."

"Best cup of coffee I've had in a long time," he declared with a grin. "I have no regrets."

"It's early yet. You might later."

She was grateful Luke wanted to help her out, but at what point would it all be too much of a hassle? When would he bail?

And why did she care so much? The truth was hard to admit.

She didn't want Luke to go anywhere. She wanted this to work out.

★　★　★

LUKE MADE A quick call to Melissa and then another to Ryan, who would now probably be up all night trying to enhance that video. God bless the guy, he never complained about not sleeping and in fact appeared to be inordinately proud of the fact he operated on about forty-five minutes a night. Personally, Luke would have been a zombie after about two days.

A second check out the front window showed the same situation with Hornsby across the street. All lights out. No movement whatsoever. He could easily get Jared or Reed to hack a database or two and find out if the neighbor was on a vacation, but he was trying to keep a low profile since the cops didn't want him a part of the investigation.

Speaking of the police...

Shaw hadn't called them about the video she'd received. Tomorrow, they'd need to go down to the station and report it, have it added to the case file. There wasn't anything actionable for the cops to do really except that it once and for all destroyed their theory that a friend had dropped in and left her a cake as a nice gesture. Which as far as Luke was concerned, was a decent enough reason to show them the video. Maybe they might get off their asses and talk to some of the people in Shaw's life.

Like Eric Bishop, for example. Luke hadn't walked out of that restaurant earlier with a good vibe. He'd been far too interested in Shaw considering they'd been broken up for months.

The headlights of a car flashed through the closed curtains. Luke peered outside and there was car in the driveway, lights on and engine running. The driver's door opened and a man stepped out, retrieved a flat box from the back seat and then jogged up to the door. A cursory inspection of the vehicle revealed a lighted sign on the roof of the car.

Before getting the text, Shaw must have ordered a pizza. Shit, with everything going on she must have forgotten all about it.

The doorbell rang and Luke opened it to a young man that looked maybe nineteen or twenty. He shoved the piping hot cardboard box at Luke, the scent of tomatoes and cheese wafting from the box.

I forgot dinner. This smells good.

"Pizza for Parker. A large with extra cheese and sausage."

Luke could eat that. He was more of a pepperoni and mushroom type but at this point he wasn't going to be picky. It was a big box for Shaw alone, though. She must have been planning leftovers for tomorrow.

"How much do I owe you?"

Luke reached for his wallet in his back pocket, but the young man shook his head. "It's all paid for."

Pulling a few stray bills out, he handed the delivery guy a tip. "Then this is for you."

"Thanks, man. Have a good night."

Luke closed the door behind him and sniffed at the box. His stomach growled in anticipation. He wouldn't dig in without talking to Shaw, however. It was her pizza and she hadn't planned on him showing up tonight.

Dressed and ready to go, Shaw came out to the living room with a small bag in her hand.

"Did I hear the doorbell?"

Luke held up the box. "It was the pizza you ordered."

Her brows pinched together, Shaw frowned. "I didn't order a pizza. It must be a mistake."

"He said Parker. A large with sausage and extra cheese."

"That's my name and my usual pizza but I didn't order anything. Maybe their computer system had a glitch."

"Then they glitched with your credit card because the delivery guy said it was paid for. You might want to call them."

"I'll have to do that but at least we can enjoy the pizza. I wasn't hungry earlier, but I am now. I'll get us a couple of plates."

Luke followed Shaw into the kitchen and placed the cardboard box on the island. Shaw pulled down two plates from the cabinet and handed one to him before flipping open the box.

"It smells delicious–" She broke off, her gaze riveted to the contents of the box. "Shit…"

One large pizza. In a heart shape.

This was no accident. No glitch. Luke was certain this was deliberate.

This was a gift from her stalker.

CHAPTER SEVENTEEN

S HAW SHOULD BE sleeping. The illuminated numbers on the clock on the nightstand said it was two in the morning. All sane people were fast asleep so they could start their day in a few hours, bright-eyed and bushy-tailed. Or at least not a complete wreck.

But she wasn't going to fall asleep. She'd realized that about thirty minutes ago so instead she huddled in Luke's guest room staring at the ceiling and imagining more and more outlandish scenarios in which she finally met the person stalking her. Some of them ended well, and some ended terribly. None were pleasant.

She couldn't fault Luke in all of this. After realizing that her stalker had ordered that pizza, he'd taken control immediately. He'd called the pizza parlor, but the order had been placed by computer on a guest-type account. He or she had used a credit card, but the system didn't save the card numbers unless a box was checked by the customer. It was a security feature which was great for the person putting in their credit card information but not so great for her.

Luke had stomped around her kitchen and muttered under his breath for a few minutes and then bundled her up along with her suitcase and taken her to his house. Not wanting to eat that pizza, they'd tossed it in the trash and then stopped at a drive thru on the way. Despite her earlier hunger, she'd barely touched her food. Her stomach simply wouldn't allow her to eat much.

I am thirsty though.

Slipping out of bed, she padded on bare feet into the kitchen, checking the cabinets for a glass or a mug.

They're right next to the sink. That's where I would have put them.

Filling the glass from the dispenser in the refrigerator door, she turned around to find two curious canines staring at her. Tails wagging, tongues lolling out.

"Oh…hey guys. I didn't know you were awake."

Shaw had never had a dog before. They'd seemed quite friendly when she and Luke had arrived, giving her kisses and wanting pets, but she hadn't realized that they might follow her around the house.

"Dogs have superhero hearing. They heard you get out of bed."

Luke's voice came from around the corner and then he was standing in the kitchen wearing a pair of blue and white striped pajama pants and nothing else.

He looked good, even in the dark. Considering everything that had happened she shouldn't be noticing how hot he was. But it was a nice distraction.

"They're staring at me."

He flipped on the light and she blinked for a moment, her eyes adjusting to the sudden glare.

"You're standing next to the treat jar. They want a treat."

She was? Was she supposed to give them one? Didn't they have to sit or roll over or something to get it?

"I'll let them out in the back yard real quick and then give them one."

She stepped aside so the dogs could scamper out of the back door. Luke watched them and then after a few minutes let out a whistle that had the two canines running inside. He made them sit politely for their treat which looked like a small, flat piece of hamburger. Dylan and Murphy wolfed it down as if it were chateaubriand.

"They really like those."

"They love them. They're both very food-motivated, especially Murphy. Because of that they were pretty easy to train."

It was two in the morning and they were both avoiding the real subject. She might as well bite the bullet and get it out in the open.

"I couldn't sleep so I got up to get a glass of water."

He leaned a hip against the counter. "I figured that. I wasn't sleeping so great either. We could watch a movie if you want."

Shaw didn't want to watch a movie. She didn't know what she wanted to do.

Wait...that wasn't true. She wanted to sleep. She was exhausted but every time she closed her eyes she saw that stupid birthday cake or that creepy pizza. She could hear in her head all of the messages she'd received.

She wanted to scream in anger and frustration.

"You don't want to watch a movie. I can tell from your expression."

Groaning, Shaw tossed back the last of her water. "I want to sleep, but I don't think that's going to happen. I feel like I could jump out of my skin."

Luke rubbed the back of his neck. "Listen, I'm going to throw out a suggestion. It's just an idea. I'm not trying anything, okay? I'm thinking that it might help, that's all, and if you think it's a terrible idea I'll drop the whole subject."

"Okay..."

Was he going to suggest that she take something pharmaceutical to help her fall asleep?

"You could sleep with me. I mean, in my bed. I wouldn't try anything. It's just that sometimes it helps if you're not alone. Jesus, this sounds bad. Forget I said anything."

His cheeks were stained pink and his gaze was on his bare toes. It was cute that he was so nervous about what was actually a decent suggestion. It would make her feel more secure to have him next to her. She certainly felt safe whenever he was close by.

"I don't want to forget your offer. I think I'll take you up on it, if it's still okay."

"It is," he agreed readily. "I just don't want you to feel pressured or anything."

She didn't feel pressured. She felt relieved.

"I'm not too proud to admit that I didn't like sleeping alone. Thank you for making the offer. Even if I don't sleep, I think I'll feel more secure with you."

Without another word, Luke rinsed out her glass and then turned off the light. They walked back down the hall side by side and then paused when they were standing next to his bed.

"Which side of the bed to you prefer?" he asked. "It doesn't matter to me."

It didn't really matter to her either. A quick glance at the bed told her that he slept on the right side. The pillow had a deep indent in it and the covers were slightly more messy.

"How about the left side? Is that okay?"

"That's fine," he assured her. "Do you need an extra blanket or anything?"

Their conversation was almost comical. They were both so nervous and stilted.

"I'm fine." Wanting to break the tension, she took a leap and landed in a heap on the bed. When she looked up, he was smiling. Thank goodness. She had a weird sense of humor, but it was okay with him. "Comfy. This is nice."

The bed was huge actually, which wasn't a surprise. A regular-sized mattress wouldn't be large enough for him and another person.

"I bought it brand new about a year ago." He slid in next to her, pulling the covers up over her so she wouldn't get cold. "I've wanted a king-sized mattress my whole life."

"It's very nice."

Damn, that tension was still there, thicker than ever because now they were lying in bed together. Despite how wide the mattress was they were still touching. They couldn't help it. Luke wasn't a small man.

"Do you want me to leave the light on?"

"No, it's fine. You can turn it off."

She was too keyed up to sleep but she wasn't scared. Not with Luke and the dogs there.

Turning onto her side so her back was to him, she tucked the covers under her chin and closed her eyes. If she could simply relax a little, she was sure she could fall asleep now, all warm and cozy in Luke's bed. She could smell his scent on the sheets and she took in a lungful, citrus and spice.

But sleep didn't come.

She was hyper aware of him next to her. His breathing, every time he shifted, even the warmth from his body that had begun to seep to her side of the bed. It was maddening. Was he feeling it too? The sexual tension between them had been there from pretty much their first meeting, but tonight it was off the charts.

"Luke?"

"Hmmm?"

"Are you awake?"

"Yes, I'm awake. Are you okay?"

"I'm okay."

That wasn't the truth.

"Actually, I…do you think you could hold me?"

She didn't think he'd turn her down. That wasn't the reason

for her nervousness. It was that this was a big step forward.

They probably weren't going to just cuddle tonight.

"Of course, honey." He slid the few inches between them, spooning her from behind. It was amazing to be held so close and protectively. Her fingers wrapped around his arm, and she snuggled back against him. All of him. "Is this better?"

His voice sounded strangled. When she'd moved into him that meant she could feel every inch of him. There was a heck of a lot to feel too. He was hot and hard, his cock pressing against her bottom.

"Much better. How about you? Is this okay?"

"It's great. Awesome. Do you think you can sleep now?"

Could she? Possibly. Did she want to? No.

"I don't think I want to sleep at the moment."

"We can–"

"Luke," she interrupted, keeping her voice soft even though there was no one to hear them. Except the dogs, of course. "I think we should make love."

There. Out in the open. She'd stepped off the cliff and hoped that the landing wouldn't be too bad. He wanted her, he couldn't hide that, but did he *want* to want her? That was the question.

There was a long silence and then she felt a rumble in his chest pressed so closely to her back. He was laughing. "I like your style, Shaw. Straight and to the point. Put it all right out there. No games."

"Let's face it, Brewster. That tension-filled polite chitchat could have lasted for hours. I don't want to waste the time. Do you?"

"No, I do not."

Then his lips were on traveling across her cheek and down her neck while his hands were tracing her curves. He cupped her breasts over her t-shirt, his thumbs strumming the peaked nipples underneath. Squirming at the sensation, she ground her bottom against his cock, ripping a deep groan from his throat.

"You're evil, woman."

"I'm just getting started."

So was he, apparently. His hands slipped underneath her t-shirt to stroke the sensitive skin underneath. She shivered and sighed, flames licking at her quivering flesh. He was far too good at this. His hand slipped between her thighs and under the edge of her panties, his fingers tracing the folds before coming to rest on her clit.

She moved restlessly against him, trying to find the perfect amount of friction as he rubbed circles around the swollen pearl. The temperature of the bedroom had risen into the tropical zone and she kicked off the covers, wanting to be rid of the clothes that separated them. She wanted to feel him against her, skin to skin. Tugging at her shirt, she pulled it over her head and tossed it away. Her panties followed quickly after. Now all that was left was his pajama pants. Her fingers went to the tie in the front but then she paused, a thought occurring to her.

"Do you normally wear pajamas or did you do this for me?"

"For you," he snorted with a laugh. "I usually sleep naked,

but if you had a nightmare or something and I had to come running I didn't want to scare you."

"Don't ever wear these again."

It really was a crime to cover up his beautiful male body. He helped her strip him out of the pants and leaned down to capture her lips with his in a soul-searing kiss. She could hear her blood pumping in her veins and the heat rising all around her. When they broke apart, he nudged her back onto the mattress, his mouth and tongue teasing a rose-tipped breast. Her fingers curled into his hair and then she ran her hand down his torso, enjoying the feel of his ridged muscles underneath her palm.

When she arrived at her destination, she wrapped her hand around his length, running her hand up and down. His hand immediately clamped down over hers.

"Easy there, honey. I'm already pretty keyed up and I'd hate to bring our evening to an abrupt ending." He began to kiss his way down her torso. "Let me–"

She wanted him. She didn't want to wait any longer. Grabbing at his arms, she pulled him back up so they were nose to nose, his warm breath on her cheek.

"I need you. Now."

Groaning, he flung out an arm toward the nightstand. "You're going to be the death of me but I love it. Once again, just straight and to the–"

"Luke, for heaven's sake. Concentrate."

He could tell her how wonderful she was later. Right now, she had a one-track mind.

Feverish, she moved underneath him, rubbing against him like a cat in heat and making it almost impossible for him to put on the condom. In the end, she had to help him while they both giggled, their fingers fumbling in the half-light.

She thought he'd settle on top of her but to her surprise he sank down on the mattress next to her and gently nudged her onto her side so they were spooning again. He pulled her top leg up and back over his own and his cock pressed into her until he was in to the hilt. His fingers took up residence on her already swollen clit while his other hand slid under her and cupped her breast.

Oh, this is nice. This position is pure genius.

His lips were caressing her shoulder, his fingers dancing over her clit, and his fingers plucking at her nipples. All the while he lazily thrust in and out, deep and hard, running over all the sensitive spots until she was panting hard and couldn't see straight. Her abdomen tightened with arousal as she climbed higher and higher, ready to soar among the clouds. She was so close. It wouldn't take much more.

His teeth nibbled at the hollow of her neck near her collar-bone, an erogenous zone for her, and that was all it took to send her over the edge. Lights danced behind her lids as wave after wave ran through her limbs, all the way down to her curled toes. Luke reached his peak right after and she forced herself to turn and watch him as his orgasm overtook him. His head was thrown back and his jaw was clamped together. He was a gorgeous man and never more so than this moment.

When it was all over and their damp bodies had cooled, Luke lifted her up and carried her into the bathroom so they could get clean under the steamy shower. He had to hold her up, her legs were still jelly but they managed without any major mishaps. Afterward he tenderly dried her with a fluffy towel and then tucked her back under the covers, once again spooning her from behind.

Her body almost boneless, she began to drift off to sleep, safe and warm in Luke's strong arms. He'd become so important to her in such a short time. She hadn't expected this to happen, hadn't even really wanted it to, but there they were.

Shaw was falling in love with this man. This amazing, wonderful man.

CHAPTER EIGHTEEN

W HEN THEY WENT to speak to the police the next morning it was far different than the first time. This time they took Shaw much more seriously. They couldn't blame a random friend for breaking into her home and leaving the cake, although one of the officers tried, saying that perhaps the cake and the video were an elaborate prank. She'd replied that none of her friends had that sort of sense of humor and neither did she.

Since they still didn't know who was doing this, the officer in charge had promised to send a patrol by her house three or four times a day in hopes of perhaps catching a glimpse at her intruder or at the least intimidating him if he was hanging around.

The cop did seem to think that she had done the right thing installing cameras and security, and he'd been almost nice to Luke when he'd said it. At the end, he'd apologized that they couldn't do more for her. She'd appreciated his obvious sincerity, and he had acted professionally, making sure that the entirety of her situation was documented. He'd said that she might need all of this information if the man was eventually caught.

If. That was a little word with a big question.

Luke appeared to be confident. He'd assured her that now that her stalker was becoming bolder and escalating it would only be a matter of time before they could catch him on camera. After all, he wouldn't know that she'd installed a security system.

On the way back to Shaw's house, they'd grabbed a coffee and a muffin, hoping to fuel up for the day ahead. Despite all the turmoil going on in her life, she had to work. She couldn't simply throw up her hands and give into the stress. She did think getting her mind off her own problems might help her too. Better to concentrate on other people than to wallow in her own quagmire of crap.

Speaking of crap... Shaw's phone chimed with a text message. Someone or something had set off her doorbell camera.

"Something set off the camera," she said, pulling up the app to see. "It might just be the postman though."

Could they get lucky enough to catch her intruder on the first full day with her new security system?

Nope, and she wasn't lucky at all. One glimpse at the car in the driveway on the video and she wanted to beat her head against the car window.

Her mother's car was in her driveway unexpectedly. Again.

"It's my mom and stepfather," Shaw said. They turned the corner to her street. Was it too late to turn around and go elsewhere? Probably. "I'm not going to tell them about the video."

"Then I won't either," Luke promised. "I'll take my cues from you."

"You can say anything you want, just don't tell them about the video. I don't want my mother to have a stroke. Even a pretend one."

Julia had thought several times that she was having a stroke or a heart attack because of something that Shaw had done or said. In reality, she was as healthy as a horse.

"Can I ask you a question? Do they do this a lot? Just show up at your house without calling or anything?"

"Yes," she answered promptly and with a heavy sigh. "And I hate it. I keep telling her that they need to call or text, but she insists that she's my mother and that this is normal. Is it normal?"

Pulling into the driveway next to her parents' car, Luke could only shrug. "I don't know what's normal. I only know that my family is big on calling first, but that could just be us. Have you asked your friends? I could ask some of mine."

"I have. Most of them say that it's not normal but a few say that it is. I think it might be family specific. Either way, my mom is standing on my front lawn."

More specifically, Julia was standing in the middle of Shaw's front lawn, her hands on her hips, and wearing a scowl. She wasn't happy.

Tough, Mom. I'm not happy today either. You need to wait your turn.

Julia must have found out her key didn't work anymore.

Luke and Ryan had changed the locks on the house because of the stalker. The fact that Shaw's mother couldn't just let herself in whenever she wanted was a bonus.

"Gird your loins," Shaw joked as she pushed open the car door. "This isn't going to be pleasant."

"I've got your back."

He might but he'd never come up against Shaw's mother. She had a way of twisting everything until it didn't resemble anything even remotely real.

Julia stomped up to Shaw and pulled her into a hug. "Shaw, we were worried sick. Where have you been? And why doesn't my key work?"

Shaw held up her paper coffee cup and the half-eaten muffin. "We went to get a bite of breakfast. Mom, what are you doing here?"

"I'm here to see you, of course. Oliver and I are looking at a house a few neighborhoods over and we wanted you to see it with us. It has a lovely mother-in-law suite that would be perfect for you."

Not today. I can't take this today.

"I am not moving out of my house, Mother. That wouldn't make any sense."

Shaw tried to keep her tone level and friendly, but it was no use. She sounded shaky and pissed off. Which she was. But Mom didn't need to know that. Thank goodness, Julia wasn't noticing anything about Shaw this morning, too into her own drama.

"It's not safe for you here. Your home was broken into."

"I don't think that's a good enough reason to sell my house. We talked about this, remember? And that's why your key doesn't work. We changed the locks."

Shaw opened the front door so they could all go inside out of the chilly weather.

"I can make coffee," she offered. "Or some iced tea."

Julia was in no mood for refreshments. Apparently, she'd climbed out of her bed and decided to make life difficult for her daughter today.

"I still think that you should stay with us for awhile, Shaw," her mother said, giving the back door a disdainful look. "I won't be able to eat or sleep worrying about you."

There it was. The gauntlet. Julia had thrown it down like so many times before.

Will I crumble like always?

Will I let my own mother be miserable by not giving in?

Shaw glanced at Luke who, frankly, looked like he wanted to be anywhere but where he was. She didn't blame him. She'd like to be somewhere else too.

She'd had so many conversations with Melissa, Taylor, and now Luke as well. Ryan too. She certainly knew what she'd tell someone writing into her channel about this problem.

I have an issue with boundaries.

That's my problem and it's fixable.

My mother's issues aren't my problem though. Only she can change those.

Taking a deep breath, Shaw steeled herself for the storm to come.

"I am not going to stay with you, Mother. I am a grown woman."

Although sometimes I have to remind myself.

"A grown woman who would allow her own mother to be sad and tortured," Julia said, a plaintive tone in her voice. "I can't believe my own daughter cares so little for me."

Shaw was standing on the brink, her entire body quivering on the edge of the cliff. She was this close to jumping off and giving into her mother. She'd done it so many times. What would one more be? It was always easier in the moment to give Julia whatever she wanted. To make her happy. Those rare times that Shaw had stood her ground she'd paid for it eventually. Julia would go silent for days or even weeks, refusing to return texts, calls, or emails. She'd complain to her sisters or cousins about what a horrible daughter she had, prompting family to contact Shaw and let her know how much she'd hurt her mother. It was a merry go round that she wasn't anxious to jump on and ride.

At some point, Luke had moved to Shaw's side and had placed an arm around her shoulders. Calm and strength radiated from his person and it gave her just enough strength to hold her ground.

"I love you, Mother, but I'm not going to run home every time life gets messy or difficult. I'm sorry that you worry but I hope that by now you know you can trust me to make good decisions."

Shaw had placed it all back on her parent. If Julia said that Shaw couldn't be trusted to do the right thing, that would call into question the parenting she had received. No way was Julia going to say that she hadn't been a good role model.

"I never said that," Julia deflected. "I said that I'll worry sick about you. Don't you care?"

If Shaw thought for one moment that her mother would truly not eat or sleep, she might have relented then and there. But experience had told her differently.

"I love you, Mom, and of course I care about you."

The spindly little twig fence that Shaw had built was wavering in the breeze. A good gust of wind could knock it down, but she had to believe that this boundary would hold.

Don't explain myself. Don't try and justify my behavior. Just stick to my guns.

It helped that Luke stood by her side, not jumping in to help her or explain how safe she was. He trusted her. He trusted that she could deal with this on her own.

I can.

"Well—then—I don't understand you," Julia sputtered, her cheeks pink. "You need to listen to me, Shaw. I'm your mother."

"The decision has been made."

Shaw's voice was far too quivery. She needed to toughen up.

"What did you say?"

Julia looked outraged.

"I said that the decision has been made."

This time Shaw sounded better, far more firm. Confident

even.

I can do this. I'm doing it.

Julia burst into tears and ran from the room. So much for confident and cool.

"Shaw, you need to go after your mother and talk to her. She's very upset."

Oliver's tone was full of reproach. Even his expression said he was incredibly disappointed in her. How could she fix this and keep her boundaries intact?

It was time to find out.

★ ★ ★

SHAW HAD FOLLOWED her mother somewhere down the hall, probably the bathroom, leaving Luke standing in the kitchen with her stepfather Oliver. To say it was awkward would be an understatement. They both just stood there sort of looking at each other, not really knowing what to say.

The fact was Luke had a hell of a lot to say about the behavior of Shaw's mother who had no hesitation to play the guilt card when she didn't get her way. That shit wouldn't fly in the house that he'd grown up in. It would have been called out and squashed the first time she'd tried it but clearly she'd been playing on Shaw's sympathies, and probably Oliver's too, for a long time since she was currently throwing a tantrum a toddler would be proud of.

But he wasn't going to say any of it. It wasn't his damn business. If Shaw wanted his help she'd ask. Until then, he was simply a bystander. Honestly, he hoped that he'd misunderstood and everything he thought about her mother wasn't true. He'd love to have Shaw say that Julia never pulled anything like this and it was the first time ever.

"She's just trying to look out for her daughter," Oliver finally said with a small smile. "Julia is a devoted mother. She loves Shaw more than anything in the world."

Then why is she making her miserable?

"I'm sure that she does."

But Oliver wasn't done. He appeared to want to make it even more weird between them.

"We shouldn't come between a mother and her child. That's a sacred bond."

"I would never do that."

"You did, though. Installing this security system keeps Shaw from moving back with Julia."

Luke counted to ten before he replied. He'd been trying to stay out of this but they were determined to drag him into the middle.

"Shaw isn't a child. She's a grown woman who can make her own decisions. I'm not making those for her. She wanted to stay in her home and I've simply helped her do that."

He didn't mention that he had some of the same equipment at his own home.

"Do you have children, Luke?"

"No, I don't."

"Then you don't understand."

That was a possibility. Luke had never traversed these waters with anyone he'd dated. He wasn't a parent. He was Shaw's friend, and in that capacity he would stand by her.

Until she told him not to anymore.

He had a feeling that she wasn't going to come back in the kitchen a happy woman.

★　★　★

JULIA WAS SITTING on the side of the bathtub, sniffling and blowing her nose although no tears had actually fallen down her face. She wouldn't like her makeup getting messed with.

Shaw was leaning on the bathroom vanity trying desperately to convince her mother that what she was doing was totally normal. Grown children were supposed to live their own lives and make their own way in the world.

That statement had gone over like a lead balloon.

"It's him, isn't it?" Julia said, dabbing a tissue around her eyes. "It's that man. The reason you don't want to come home with me is that you're living with him."

"I'm not living with him, Mom. I live here."

"Then he's staying here," Julia said, accusation in her tone. "He's the one standing in the way. He's here so you don't have to go anywhere, right?"

"Even if Luke wasn't in my life, I wouldn't move home," Shaw replied truthfully. "I'm grown up and I've flown the nest. I have a great job that I love and a nice home. I want you to be proud of me, Mom, of the things that I've achieved."

"I've never said I wasn't proud of you. Of course, I'm proud of you. You're smart and talented and you could do so much more with your career if you really wanted to. You could go back and get your PhD."

Shaw was planning to do that eventually but not this week. Her mother, however, never missed an opportunity to bring this topic up.

"I know you hate my career, but I enjoy it."

"I don't hate it. I just think you could do better."

"It's what I've chosen to do. For now, at least."

Julia looked up at her, her expression almost angry. "And my opinion doesn't count?"

It's what Shaw had been trying to say for a long time now but in a nice way. Her mother wasn't going to let her though.

"You got to make your own decisions when you were my age. Now it's my turn."

"That's not true," Julia protested, shaking her head. "I made my decisions based on what was best for you. I always thought about you."

"Then this is your time to have what you want," Shaw pressed. "You don't have to make decisions based on me anymore. I can take care of myself. Go have fun with Oliver. Travel, make friends, get a cat. Get two cats. Live your life. What have you always wanted to do, Mom? There has to be something that you've always dreamed of."

"I don't want a cat, and I have friends. I travel and have fun. Is it so awful to want you to be a part of all of that?"

"No, but I can't always do all the things that you want me to do when you want me to do them."

Julia nodded toward the door. "Like him? You're busy with him. You know, men don't respect a woman that's too easy, Shaw. You should take things more slowly with him."

"Mom, we're not getting anywhere with this. I think we disagree on the basic premise of this discussion. I need to be independent and to be living my own life. That doesn't mean that I don't love you, it means that I'm trying to make my own way in the world. It means that I need to stand on my own two feet and make my own decisions."

"Of course, you need to be independent. But that doesn't mean that you can't take advice," Julia replied. "That we can't discuss your life."

Shaw took a deep breath. This wasn't going well.

"When we talk about my life, you make me feel like I have to do things your way."

"I'm older than you, Shaw. You should make use of my wisdom."

"I want to make my own mistakes."

Taking a shuddering breath, Julia stood and shoved the tissue into her purse. "If you're going to be stubborn and short-sighted then I don't think we have much more to say here. I'm going home. I can only hope that you think about this conversation and realize how much you're hurting me."

Shaw opened her mouth to say she was sorry, a reflexive apology that she usually said every time she was in the same room with Julia. She'd apologized all the time even for things that weren't her fault. But this time... This time she snapped her mouth shut.

In truth, she didn't think she'd done anything wrong. She'd tried to be nice about all of this but clearly that wasn't working. Julia wanted to insert herself into every aspect of Shaw's life. Shaw, on the other hand, wanted to make her own decisions and live independently. Someone was bound to come out of the situation disappointed.

As she followed her mother down the hall toward the kitchen and living room, Shaw knew one thing for sure.

This wasn't over. Her mother wasn't going to give up without a fight. This was only round one. Shaw might have found her backbone, but it was going to be tested to its limits.

CHAPTER NINETEEN

S HAW'S MOTHER AND stepfather finally left, leaving her and Luke alone. He hadn't said much and neither did she, to be honest. What was there to say? She sucked at putting up boundaries, and he'd been there to witness the debacle.

Big deal…she'd shored up her defenses and stuck to her guns. Today. What would happen tomorrow? Or the next day? Julia wasn't going to go quietly. Her mother was regrouping at the moment, figuring out what other buttons she could push to get her way.

And Luke? He must think that her family was incredibly dysfunctional – which was the truth – and questioning whether he really wanted to be involved with her at all. She wouldn't blame him if he wanted to run away far and fast.

It had taken quite a bit of persuading to get him to go to work and leave her here at the house all alone. He'd finally left but only after she'd assured him that it was broad daylight and nothing bad was going to happen to her. He'd relented but he hadn't been happy about it. He'd promised to take her out tonight to help her forget what a crappy day she was having.

And then there was the whole Vegas trip. She wanted to go but she didn't want to feel like she'd been chased away. She wanted to go and be able to let her hair down, have some fun. She wanted to be able to leave her worries behind and get to know this amazing man a little better.

Later she'd ended up in the spare bedroom that she used as a studio to film content for her channel. For a few hours, she was able to forget all her problems and get lost in her work. It felt good to be productive and somewhat normal. It was lunchtime when she took a break to get something to eat, her stomach growling loudly.

A cursory inspection of her cabinets and refrigerator had her microwaving a frozen dinner. It wasn't what she really wanted but it would have to do. She was almost finished eating when her phone began to chime with text after text. She thumbed the screen and her stomach clenched painfully at what she saw.

Another unknown number. Brand new since she'd blocked the last one that had sent the video.

This time it was message after message about how she was ignoring him and who did she think she was. Clearly, he was furious at being ignored and he promised retribution if she didn't contact him. Basically, bad shit was going to happen unless she talked to him.

It looks like bad things are going to happen then.

Shaw had to admit that it was tempting to hit the reply button. It would be so easy to give him what he wanted. Reply and tell him to leave her alone. It would only take a moment. But it wasn't the answer. It would only make the situation far worse than it already was. Replying to any of this would be the worst thing she could do.

She had to sort of laugh about it though – in a completely non-funny way. Once again, it was all about having boundaries. It was certainly the day for her to practice building them, first with her mother and then with her stalker. If this went on much longer, she was going to be a damn expert.

To keep herself from texting him back, she deliberately placed her phone out of reach and on her charger. Out of sight, out of mind. She'd already saved the messages to her folder of communications so she'd blocked this new number as well.

She headed back into the kitchen to clean up the remains of her lunch, but her phone chimed again. This time it was an alert from her security app. Someone had pulled into her driveway. The car wasn't familiar but the man that stepped out of it was. Eric Bishop – her ex. What on earth was he doing here? Didn't he get the hint that she didn't want to see him? She hadn't replied to any of his texts.

This was the worst part about some unknown human being stalking her. It made her suspicious and wary. Now she was wondering whether Eric was as harmless as she'd originally thought. Was it a coincidence that he'd appeared after she wouldn't reply to any texts? It probably was but she couldn't be sure. Not anymore. Everyone was a suspect and she hated that.

Steeling herself for the inevitable meeting, she opened the door after Eric rang the bell. He was dressed in khakis and a button-down shirt, his usual attire when he worked. Given the time of day, he might be on his way to the restaurant.

So why did he stop here?

She'd opened the door but didn't step back to let him in, instead standing in the small opening and hoping he'd take the hint that he wasn't welcome.

"Hey, Shaw. I'm sorry to just drop by but I thought we needed to talk."

Nodding, she stood her ground. She was getting to practice boundaries again.

"Eric, what are you doing here?"

"Some guy stopped by the restaurant to talk to me. He said that you're having issues with some guy–" He broke off and tried to peer over her shoulder. "Listen, this would be more comfortable if we could talk inside. Can I come in?"

Keeping on hand on the doorknob and the other on the frame, she took a small step forward.

"I don't think that would be a very good idea, actually. We can talk right here."

A flash of irritation crossed his features but then vanished as he mustered a smile.

"I just want to talk, Shaw. That's all. I'm worried about you. That guy–"

"Luke," Shaw interjected. "His name is Luke Brewster."

"Right, right. Brewster. He gave me his card." Eric reached into his breast pocket and retrieved the small white rectangle. "Anyway, he asked me if I knew anyone that might be harassing you and I told him that I didn't."

"Did you change your mind? Did you think of someone?"

He rubbed the back of his neck and shook his head. "Well…no. But it's all I've been able to think about since I talked to him and I was just so worried about you. I wanted to see you."

She didn't want to see him. He wasn't a bad person – that she knew of – but their relationship hadn't been going anywhere. They didn't have much in common and his sense of humor was far different than her own. It had been a relief to end it. They hadn't dated that long to be honest, although he had seemed to be far more optimistic about their chances than she had been.

"I don't think this is a good idea," she finally replied. "I can't see how this would help."

"I was just thinking that maybe we could have a cup of coffee. Talk a little. Maybe we'll think of someone that might be bothering you."

What do I tell my viewers? What scripts do I give them to set boundaries?

"I'm afraid that won't work for me but thank you for offering. It was very thoughtful."

"It's just a cup of coffee. Not dinner or anything."

"That's not really the point, Eric. I just don't think it's a good idea."

To her surprise, Eric threw up his hands in frustration. "I'm just trying to help you."

"And I appreciate that, but you already talked to Luke. If

you think of anything else, you can give him a call."

Pressing his lips together, he blew out a noisy breath. "You're being difficult. It's not a big deal."

Eric was the one being difficult, and frankly, Shaw was getting damn tired of people accusing her of being difficult when she wouldn't give into whatever they wanted her to do. It was really starting to piss her off.

"I don't want to argue with you."

She heard footsteps and then a shadow fell across Eric. "Shaw, is everything okay?"

James. Her neighbor from across the street who had been missing the last few days. He was standing on her porch steps scowling at her ex-boyfriend.

"Everything is fine. Eric was just leaving."

Eric opened his mouth to protest but then he simply shook his head and turned to go. "Fine, I guess I am leaving. I was just trying to help but forget it. Deal with it yourself."

With a huff, Eric stomped down the steps and jumped into his car, gunning the engine as he backed out of the driveway. The relief she felt as his departure was taken over by her trepidation at having James at her door.

"He doesn't seem like a happy man," James observed. "Are you okay?"

"I'm fine," Shaw assured him. "He came unannounced and surprised me. I don't think he'll come back. Thanks for checking on me."

Until Luke had pointed out how strange James was she'd

never given him a second thought. But now…

"You're welcome. Glad I could help. I was just going to work on replacing my mailbox. I think someone must have driven by last night and hit it accidentally. It's all dented."

She looked over James' shoulder and sure enough the post that the mailbox sat on was definitely leaning.

"That's terrible. Did you hear anything?"

"I didn't but I found it that way when I went to get my morning paper. Probably some kids did it."

Why did everyone blame kids? Shaw had never understood that. Adults did plenty of crappy stuff too.

Her first instinct was to tell him that she had a doorbell camera newly installed and that she probably had footage from last night. It might not help as she doubted that they could read the license plate, but it might be worth a shot.

Her second instinct was to shut the hell up and not tell him anything. The whole point of having hidden cameras was so that people didn't know they were being filmed. Although as Luke had pointed out, so many people had cameras now it shouldn't be a surprise.

"That's too bad," she said instead. "I'm sorry that you have to replace it."

James smiled and shrugged. "It's okay. I'm going to replace it with a nice blue one. I always meant to do it when I moved in. The white one was fine, but it always looked dirty to me."

"Blue will look nice with your house."

"Thanks, I think so. If you're sure you're okay, then I better get back to it. It's supposed to rain this afternoon."

"I heard that too. Thank you again for checking on me."

"Anytime, Shaw."

She stood in her doorway as James strode back to his own garage before closing the door and locking it behind her. This day had been far too eventful. All she'd wanted to do was get some work done but the universe was clearly against that happening. She was exhausted and catching a quick nap wasn't going to solve that problem.

Not until whomever was harassing her was caught. Then and only then, would she get a good night's sleep.

SHAW WASN'T LISTENING to anyone but that guy. He hated that guy. Always there, always comforting her. He'd moved in so quickly pretending to be a hero. She shouldn't be with him. It was wrong and she was bad. She was going to pay for that mistake. For hurting him. He wouldn't let her get away with it.

CHAPTER TWENTY

B ECAUSE SHAW'S DAY was pretty awful, Luke had planned to have an evening out with her friends. Nothing big. Just some cheeseburgers and a few laughs. He'd promised to get her home and in bed early. Which home that was going to be was still an open question.

He wouldn't mind at all if she stayed with him again, but her independent streak was a mile wide, especially after dealing with her mother and her ex today, so she might insist on staying in her own home. If she did, he'd offer to sleep on the couch after he took care of the dogs back at his place. They wouldn't be thrilled to spend the night alone, but it wouldn't be the first time. He'd worked a lot of nights as a police officer. As long as he was there bright and early to let them out and feed them breakfast, they'd be fine.

His sister Melissa had suggested a sports bar near Shaw's home that had arcade games as well. He'd also asked Ryan to join them since Taylor was bringing her boyfriend Austin. Melissa had teased him that he was trying to fix her up with his co-worker. This wasn't the first time they had met either. So far, no sparks had flown and they seemed to have a more brother and sister thing going. At least Ryan wasn't the type of guy who would lie or cheat on her. On the other hand, it would be kind of weird to have his friend date his sister.

While waiting for their food, he and Ryan ended up shooting baskets at a basketball game. Melissa, Austin, Taylor, and Shaw were shooting water pistols into a clown's mouth to race a toy car to the finish line first.

"I didn't really want to play this game," Ryan said, tossing the ball toward the hoop. "I hate basketball. I wanted to talk to you."

"So talk." It was Luke's turn to make a shot. "And I like basketball. Not as much as hockey or football, but I like it."

Ryan shrugged. "I have bad memories of gym class when I was twelve."

"Were you bullied?"

Luke couldn't quite imagine that. Ryan had an air about him that made him seem sort of...dangerous. He wasn't as big as Luke was, but he could definitely hold his own in a fight.

"Let's just say it was before my growth spurt."

Chuckling, Luke took another shot that bounced off the rim. He wasn't all that great at free throws, to be honest. "And after your growth spurt? Did they stop bullying you?"

"They did."

Typical Ryan. He never used five words when two would do the job.

"So what did you want to talk to me about?"

Ryan glanced over at the others who were talking and laughing. It looked like Melissa had won the latest race.

"Have you noticed that Austin pays your girlfriend a hell of a lot of attention?"

Kind of. Luke hadn't noticed anything strange when they'd gone out for Shaw's birthday but tonight there had been a different feeling in the group. There had been an almost imperceptible shift in the dynamics.

Somehow Austin had managed to sit next to Shaw with Luke on the other side. He'd talked to her quite a bit, asking question after question. Taylor, thank goodness, didn't seem to notice anything awry with her boyfriend since Austin hadn't completely ignored her.

Luke hadn't thought much of it because the questions were all professional-related. He'd thought that the other man wanted to get Shaw's advice about a problem but didn't want to be too obvious about it.

"He has asked her a bunch of questions tonight. What are you thinking?"

"I don't know, it was just something I noticed."

Ryan didn't bring up shit for fun. He was far too deliberate.

"You think that we should check him out?"

"It wouldn't hurt. He came into Shaw's life around the same time as the messages from what I can tell. You know how Logan and Reed feel about coincidences."

Luke felt the same way.

"Let's do a quick check on him. See if he has any skeletons in his closet. But let me tell Shaw first before we do it. I don't want to go behind her back. I told her up front about checking her neighbor and her ex."

"Just give me the word and I'll get it done."

He honestly didn't think Austin was Shaw's stalker but at this point they had to check down every path.

Before this guy got any closer to the woman that Luke was falling for. Hard.

★　★　★

THE EVENING OUT with friends was exactly what Shaw needed to lighten her mood. She'd been feeling crappy all day long but for a few minutes tonight she'd forgotten that her life was a mess.

Except for her relationship with Luke. That was going well. Almost too well. Would he eventually get tired of the circus and dump her? She wouldn't blame him. It hadn't been smooth sailing lately. When she was rid of this stalker problem, they ought to go somewhere together for a few days to celebrate. Just the two of them. Maybe that Vegas trip?

Draining her glass of ice water, Shaw leaned over to Melissa. "I'm going to run to the ladies' room. I'll be right back."

Melissa nodded and went back to listening to Taylor tell the story about her and Austin's last date at a new eatery in town. It had a turn of the century London theme and was elaborately decorated along with waiters and waitresses dressed in steam-punk outfits. Shaw made a mental note to talk to Luke about trying it out.

Making her way to the restrooms which were located at the back of the restaurant and down the hall, she quickly checked her cell phone on the way.

No new messages. What a relief.

Inside the restroom, she freshened up and put on a coat of lipstick, dropping the gold tube back into her bag. Smoothing down a stray stand of her short blonde hair, she pushed the door open to head back to the table.

But it wouldn't budge.

Assuming the damp air had made it sticky, Shaw gave it another shove with her shoulder. For a moment, she thought it was going to move but it held firm. A few more frantic pushes and she realized she was trapped in the bathroom. She couldn't get out.

But...

It was a swinging door. There was no lock on it, and it had opened just fine when she'd gone in. This shouldn't be happening. Could a door swell that much in less than five minutes? She didn't think so.

She gave the door another hard shove but the only thing she managed to do was break a sweat and probably bruise her shoulder and elbow. She was a teensy bit claustrophobic and being stuck in the small room wasn't doing her any good. She wanted out.

When she was a little girl, they'd rented a house that had a sticky back door and she'd had to kick the bottom of it to get it to open. It might be worth a try. Taking a deep breath, she lifted her leg and gave the door a swift kick with the bottom of her shoe.

It moved. A little bit. Perhaps she'd loosened it?

Once again, she put her shoulder against the door and felt it slightly budge from its position. She was sure it was going to swing open, but then…it felt like someone had pushed it closed again.

This was crazy. She wasn't going to stand in this little bathroom all night pushing at a door that wasn't moving. She'd simply text Luke to help her. As big as he was, he ought to be able to pull the door open from the other side easily.

Retrieving her phone from her handbag, Shaw noticed that she'd received a text. She hadn't heard the chime because the restaurant was so loud with the games and diners.

Another unknown sender.

This time he'd sent pictures. Of her and her friends. Eating dinner inside the restaurant. Her heart instantly sped up and she frantically tapped out a text to Luke. Dammit, this was their chance to find him.

He was here.

★   ★   ★

THE SON OF a bitch was here. Or at least he had been, long enough to take pictures and send them to Shaw.

When Luke had received her text, he'd ran to help her without even stopping to explain to the others. By the time he'd arrived at the ladies' room, Shaw had managed to get out. A cursory inspection of the door showed that it had never been stuck. It swung freely out toward the hallway. Someone must have been holding it shut.

To fuck with her. To scare her.

Ryan had, of course, been right on his heels and now the two of them along with Melissa, Shaw, Taylor, and Austin were searching the restaurant and the parking lot for...what exactly? They didn't know what he looked like. Luke had hoped that Shaw might see someone that was familiar but so far she hadn't. Basically, he'd hoped that he'd see someone running away or acting suspiciously. But he hadn't. They'd come up empty. Again.

He'd been so close though. Was he one of the waiters or busboys? Had he been a customer at the loud table where all the guys were drinking beer and eating platters of wings? Did he even come into the dining area or did he stay out in the foyer near the hostess stand and the bathroom?

"Fuck," Luke muttered under his breath. He was tired of this shit. Tired of being made to look like an idiot, and he was really fucking tired of this guy preying on Shaw and scaring her. She didn't deserve this shit. "Fuck it all."

"That's eloquent."

"Fuck off, Ryan. I'm pissed right now."

"I get it and you should be."

"I know."

"So be pissed and then get the hell over it. We have work to do."

Ryan could be calm and businesslike because he wasn't emotionally involved. Which was kind of pissing off Luke even more.

"This guy—"

"Is going to get caught eventually," Ryan interrupted. "He's moving closer, taking more chances. Eventually he's going to fuck up and when he does, we'll be there. Right?"

"I want him now," Luke growled. Melissa and Taylor were comforting Shaw, doing his job for him. He should be over there taking care of her, but he had to deal with this shit first. "He's starting to get on my nerves. Can you believe it? He was here right under our noses."

"We know something about him that we didn't know before. He can blend in really well. That means he's an average guy. He doesn't stand out. I talked to the hostess to see if she noticed anyone taking pictures and she didn't. She didn't see or talk to anyone out of the ordinary."

"I'm not sure how that helps us."

"It gives us a few clues that confirm your suspicions. Look at the demographics. Mostly male because there's a ton of games and there's sports on the television. Looks like about age thirty to sixty. Your theory about the stalker being a male sounds spot on."

"The majority of stalkers are men."

"And the majority of people in this restaurant are men. If it was a woman, she would probably stand out more. Melissa, Taylor, and Shaw are currently the only females here unless you count the two adolescents with their dad playing video games. I have to believe that the hostess would have noticed another woman. We now know something that we didn't before."

"You have a point," Luke conceded. "So it's likely that it's a male. But we don't know anything more."

"We can talk to the manager. Ask for any security footage."

Luke nodded, his mind already racing forward. If they could catch this guy on video, they might be able to run him through facial recognition and get a name.

It wasn't much but it was something. He needed every advantage he could get and then some. He was getting sick and tired of dealing with this asshole. It was time to shut him down and get him out of Shaw's life. For good.

CHAPTER TWENTY-ONE

S HAW WASN'T SURE what she was supposed to feel after what had happened tonight but right now she was mad. Angry. Furious, really. She was tired of all the damn drama and the games. If she could confront her stalker at this moment, she'd scream at him that this was wrong. He couldn't just get what he wanted by forcing her hand.

It wouldn't do any good though. Because he already knew that what he was doing was wrong. He knew because he was hiding his identity. He wasn't exactly proud of it but he was doing it anyway. She understood that she wasn't an actual *person* to this man with thoughts and feelings of her own. She was an object, a symbol. She might as well be a doll or a houseplant.

She might be the focus of his attention but this was truly all about him, and the way he felt about himself. Knowing it, however, didn't make it any easier. It was difficult to step back from her own emotionally charged situation and be cold and analytical. This was her life, her freedom. She didn't feel like she could go anywhere or do anything without him...watching.

It was creepy as fuck, to be blunt. It was as if she could feel his gaze on her all the time. And she didn't even know who he was.

Melissa and Taylor had done their best to comfort her tonight but they couldn't change the nasty fact that someone was following her, bent on making every day a nightmare.

Unless she gave him her attention. She wasn't going to do that.

Eventually, Austin had offered to drive Melissa home along with Taylor, Ryan had headed back to the office to try and get footage from nearby traffic cameras, and Luke had driven her home so she could pack another bag. He'd been quite adamant that he didn't want to leave her alone tonight. She hadn't argued.

"He certainly has a lot of time on his hands," Shaw remarked sarcastically while Luke made them hot chocolate in his kitchen. Dylan and Murphy were curled at her feet protectively, and she had to admit that she did feel better when they were here. All three of them – Luke and the two canines. "He should probably get a hobby or a job."

"You know how this works," Luke replied, pouring the steaming cocoa into two mugs. It smelled delicious even with her unsettled tummy. "You are his hobby and job. You're his whole world right now. Tomorrow morning, I'm going to check your car for a tracker and your house for listening devices."

Holy hell. Had it come to that? It had, apparently.

"Listening devices? Trackers? You have to be joking."

Now she really was sick to her stomach, the hot chocolate

tasting bitter on her tongue.

"I wish I was, but he's already shown us he's at least a little tech savvy by switching profiles and IP addresses. There are tons of websites where he could get a car tracker and he had the opportunity to plant listening devices when he was in your home. I'm just pissed off at myself because I didn't think to do it before."

"You didn't know he was going to do this."

"I should have known. It's my goddamn job to know."

Luke sounded as frustrated as she felt.

"Don't do this to yourself. It can't be easy dealing with this when you're involved. It's easier when you're just an innocent bystander. I'm having an issue with it myself, so I understand."

"Ryan is right," Luke ground out between gritted teeth. "He's going to mess up eventually. We thought it might have been tonight. We asked the manager for security footage so we could run facial recognition, but it turns out he's anti-technology. Doesn't have any cameras, for fuck's sake. He may be the last remaining public establishment that doesn't have any cameras. He kept talking about privacy concerns and the government looking over his shoulder. I get it but dammit, I wanted that video."

"What do we do in the meantime?"

Rubbing his chin, Luke shook his head. "I have a few ideas but I'm not sure if they're any good. I want to run them by Logan and Reed, get their input. We do know that his guy is escalating, moving closer to you. That's in our favor."

"Funny how it doesn't feel that way on my end."

His lips twisted in sympathy. "I know but it is good. He's not acting so controlled anymore. He's becoming erratic. That stunt with the bathroom door tonight? It was childish as hell, first of all, and second it was stupid. He could have been seen by anyone walking by. He's getting sloppy and that's exactly what we need."

With everything going on tonight, she'd completely forgotten about tomorrow.

Shit. Shit. Shit.

"Luke, I have that meet and greet tomorrow."

She'd told him about it before so he was aware, but he'd probably forgotten the date as well.

"Can you cancel? I'm not sure it's safe."

She shook her head. "Not this late, and not unless I was in bed with the flu. They're depending on me to be there. I can't let them down."

It was her job and she took it seriously.

"Then I'll be there too. Hell, maybe he'll show up. Your subscribers know about this?"

"They do."

"Then maybe we'll get lucky. I'll ask Ryan to help as well."

"I'm not sure I would classify my stalker showing up at my meet and greet as lucky."

"We need to see his face. That will change everything. Ryan and I won't let him get anywhere near you. We'll be watching the entire time."

It did make her feel better that they would be there.

Speaking of watching...

Her gaze drifted to the window where the drapes were pulled shut. "Do you think he's...?"

She couldn't say the words because she didn't want it to be true.

Luke placed his mug on the kitchen counter and walked over to her, pulling her into his warm, strong arms. This. Right here. This was what she'd been wanting all evening. Being with her friends was wonderful but luxuriating in Luke's arms made her feel safe and protected. A status she wasn't feeling much these days.

"I'm not going to let anything happen to you," he said, his lips grazing her forehead as if she were a child. She'd been whiny enough lately to qualify as one and she was exhausted from being unhappy. She was an optimist normally. "You're safe here with us. No one is going to get to you."

She believed him. But...

"You didn't actually answer my question. Do you think he's out there right now? Watching us?"

"If he is, all he's going to get is pneumonia from freezing his ass off. If he comes close the dogs are going to lose their shit. Murphy barks if a squirrel farts in the backyard. He won't get within thirty feet of the house."

"That doesn't stop him from watching."

Creepy. Creepy.

"No, but it makes getting close to you a hell of a lot more

difficult. My number one job is to keep you safe while I catch this guy."

Slumping against him, she laid her head on his chest. His heart beat strong and steady underneath her ear. "What if you don't catch him?"

"We'll get him. Please trust me."

She trusted Luke. She had to. The alternative was far too awful to contemplate.

★ ★ ★

SHAW WAS FINALLY asleep. It had taken two hot chocolates and Luke giving her a long back rub while the television had played in the background, but she'd eventually succumbed, her eyelids fluttering shut just a few minutes past midnight. She had to be exhausted and he hoped she'd sleep through the night.

He, on the other hand, was far too restless. She'd brought up a damn good point earlier when they'd been talking about what had happened.

Are you out there, asshole?

Lifting the edge of the curtain, he peered out onto his front yard. He'd purposely left on his porch light and the lights above his garage and back doors as well. If Shaw's stalker was out there, Luke wasn't about to make it easy for him.

Dylan nudged at Luke's hand, his snout pushing the curtain slightly farther aside so he could see outside too. The canine had to be wondering what was up with his dad. Normally they'd all be sprawled out asleep at this time of night, Luke on his bed and the dogs on their huge cushions only a few feet away.

"Where's your brother, little buddy?" he crooned to Dylan, giving him a loving scratch behind the ear. "Is he snoozing?"

The dog whined and pushed his head under Luke's finger, begging to be petted.

"You knew I was patrolling the house, huh? You had to be part of that. Well, what do you think, Dylan? Do you hear or see anything? Is Daddy getting paranoid?"

The canine tilted his head as if trying to decipher the whispered words. Eventually he decided that a tail wag was his answer.

All was right in the world, according to Dylan. If he didn't hear anything, then there was no one out there.

Right now. But later? This bastard wasn't going to give up, and Luke would be waiting for him.

★ ★ ★

SHAW'S LIDS FLUTTERED open, awareness returning slowly as she yawned and stretched, squirming into a more comfortable position. Somehow she'd managed to get some sleep last night, pure exhaustion being the only reasonable explanation. She'd assumed that she'd have horrible nightmares but instead she'd slept hard, which was making it more difficult to wake up this morning.

And it was morning. Light filtered through the blinds, letting her know that the sun had been up for more than a few minutes. Reaching out for her phone on the nightstand, she checked the time. Eight o'clock.

Turning over, she looked at the man that had become so important to her in such a short amount of time. Right now his features were soft and relaxed in sleep, but last night he'd been furious. Yet he remained controlled at the same time. She couldn't say that she hated his protective mode either. With any other guy that she had dated in the past she would have railed against it, crying out about how capable she was and that she didn't need anyone's help.

Luke didn't make her feel less because of this situation. He was so calm and matter of fact. As in *of course you need help getting rid of a stalker.* Everyone would. *Of course, you're scared.* Everyone would be.

He was almost too handsome. Not in a pretty boy sort of way. Only inches away from his face, she could see that his nose was slightly crooked, possibly from being broken in the past. He'd told her that he'd played sports in high school so it could have happened then. His jaw was strong and square and those lashes… Why was it that men seemed to have the longest and thickest lashes while women spent half their lives putting on mascara?

She was so lost in studying him that she was surprised when his eyes popped open and a smug smile crossed his face.

"Are you staring at me, Shaw Parker?"

He didn't sound mad. Actually his voice was a little gravelly and it sent a tingle down her spine.

"Why on earth would I stare at you?"

"Because I'm so good-looking."

Sputtering, she rolled her eyes but managed to scoot even closer to him so she could feel the heat from his body. "I can see that humility isn't a thing with you. Arrogant much?"

"It isn't arrogance if it's true."

"It is arrogance. Do women tell you you're good-looking or is it something that you've always just known deep down?"

His shoulders shook with laughter as he lifted her hand to press a soft kiss onto the palm.

"I only care if you think I'm good-looking."

It wasn't an answer to her question, but it sounded just fine.

"You're…adequate."

Next thing she knew she was flat on her back staring up at a very handsome and aroused male.

Lucky me.

"Adequate, huh? That's a little hurtful, Shaw. I find you so much more than adequate."

He did? She wanted to explore that further. For a few minutes she wanted to forget the outside world and simply be close to Luke. As close as possible, to be specific.

Running her fingertips across his biceps, she rubbed the sole of her foot against his leg.

"Why don't you remind me just how much better than adequate you are? With everything going on, I get so forgetful."

With an evil grin he leaned down and pressed a kiss to her lips, then to her jaw and ear, then finally at the base of her neck where her pulse was beating frantically. It hadn't taken much to raise her temperature and now the bedroom was hotter than hell.

"How could you forget this?" he asked, running his tongue across her collarbone and then nipping at the flesh of her shoulder. She quivered and sighed as his hand glided down her back to cup her bottom. "Or this? Was it really so unmemorable?"

"Maybe not completely forgotten," she choked out as his tongue encircled an already rock-hard nipple. Her fingers curled into his soft, springy hair, desperate to pull him closer. "Don't stop."

"I'm just getting started."

Shaw's heart thumped against her rib cage as Luke placed open-mouthed kisses down her abdomen, each one setting off a shower of sparks against her damp skin.

"Yes," she hissed as his tongue traced patterns on the sensitive flesh of her inner thigh. "More."

Chuckling at her demands, he didn't argue, exploring every intimate nook and cranny until she was panting, her back arched off the mattress. A coil of arousal was tightening in her belly, inexorably pulling her closer to the edge until she was teetering on the brink, ready to explode at any second.

When her orgasm did hit only moments later, she dug her nails into Luke's shoulders as she rode out each intoxicating wave of pleasure. Hot lava flew in her veins and she called out his name in a strangled voice that she barely recognized as her own.

Still floating on her sparkly cloud of pleasure, she barely registered him fumbling in the drawer next to the bed, but she heard the crinkle of foil and then he was there, exactly where she needed him to be. He pressed in slowly, letting them both savor the moment until he'd pushed all the breath from her body and all she could do was cling to him like a ship in a storm.

"Ready, baby?"

Wrapping her legs around his lean middle, she pressed kisses to his chest and shoulders, everywhere she could reach. His skin tasted salty and she swiped at his skin with her tongue. His strokes started out languid and sweet as if they had no place to be that morning and no one to answer to. Only the two of them existed in their world. Their gazes met and locked as his thrusts sped up, their urgency building as they both climbed toward their peak.

"Can you?"

His question was bit out between clenched teeth. His jaw was tight and his expression raw and primal, only serving to amp up her own arousal ten-fold. She loved that she could make him feel that way, and that he had to work so hard to keep himself in check. One day she was going to take great pleasure in helping him lose just a little bit of that control.

"I can. I just need…"

She didn't have to finish her plea because his fingers were on her swollen clit, circling and teasing until her climax slammed into her, sending her flying into outer space complete with shooting stars and fireworks. Luke followed her off the cliff, his face tucked into the crook of her neck, and his warm breath caressing her shoulder.

Eventually they collapsed on the bed, both smiling and giggling, still wrapped in their warm and comfy cocoon. At some point, they'd have to face the real world but for now they'd simply enjoy lying close, their damp skin pressed together and their breathing ragged from their exertions.

But for now, she'd cuddle close and pretend that all was right in her world.

CHAPTER TWENTY-TWO

THE MEET AND greet for Shaw's subscribers was located at a downtown Seattle restaurant for lunch. She'd made reservations weeks ago when she had the final count and the management had helpfully offered up a small back room for the gathering, which would be far more private and much quieter.

She was nervous but excited, looking forward to meeting some of the people that had been following her channel, many from the very beginning. She'd done several of these meet and greets, one as far away as New York City, and it was always fun and interesting. At no time did she feel uncomfortable or threatened.

Let's hope it's that way today too.

Luke was with her, of course. He had hopes that perhaps the stalker might show up even to just watch the get together from afar. Ryan had staked out a spot in the main dining room and was currently flirting with a pretty waitress and ordering mountains of food that would hopefully keep anyone from getting suspicious as to why he was sitting there far longer than usual.

The guests had trickled in, but she now had a full house. She greeted each one and took a selfie with them if they asked. She tried to give every one of them some individual attention. She would have done it no matter what, but Luke had encouraged it as well. He wanted her to engage with each of them in case anyone said something suspicious or behaved strangely.

This part of her job didn't come the most naturally to Shaw. She was often uncomfortable meeting new people, but her agent had assured her that she needed to have a more personal touch with her fans since they saw her exclusively online. Her first meet and greet had almost been torture but now she had a system for how she dealt with it. She'd learned to relax and enjoy herself.

They all had ordered their drinks and the restaurant had placed a buffet on the far wall that smelled delicious. Shaw encouraged everyone to fill their plates, relax, and eat.

There were about twenty people and the restaurant staff had set up the rectangular tables in a U-shape so that everyone could see each other and be heard. Luke took a chair in the corner near the door and tried to be inconspicuous, which he couldn't be if he threw a sheet over his head that matched the wallpaper. The group was mostly female and every single one of them had looked him up and down, a few of them making it obvious that they were enjoying the view.

After their stomachs were full, Shaw started the question and answer section of the meet and greet. This was honestly her favorite part of these events. Most of the questions were about their personal problems, although one or two were about Shaw in particular, such as if she was married or in a relationship, did she have children, what made her start her channel, what her future plans were. Harmless stuff. Generally, only super fans were going to take a few hours out of their day to have lunch with a channel creator.

The questions started out with the usual – roommate drama, toxic relationships, making friends, and one extremely concerned woman who was dating a guy with three cats. She was allergic to cats. Did they have a future together?

Shaw's friend Taylor was allergic to cats and she had two of them. She liked them more than she hated to blow her nose. She took medicine every single day and Shaw had never once heard her friend complain about it. Taylor just loved kitties and she was going to have them as long as they didn't kill her. Not knowing the extent of the woman's allergies, however, Shaw crafted a more middle of the road response – asking if medication helped.

The woman named Marcie shook her head. "I haven't found one yet that really helps. I can't breathe and I get rashes."

"That sounds like a deal breaker to me," Shaw replied. Her policy was to always be honest but to temper it with care. "Is he a real cat person? Or did he maybe just end up with them because a roommate moved out and left the cats behind?"

Marcie's lips turned down. "He's a real cat person. He loves them. He even dresses them up in little outfits and takes their picture. He puts the photos up on social media."

How do the cats feel about that?

"If you really think that he's the one, then you owe it to yourself to get a new allergist who might be able to help you. I don't know enough about the subject to tell you if it will do any good, but I think you have to know that deep down you did all you could. As for him, well, if he loves his cats it wouldn't be fair to ask him to give them up. I'm one of those who believes that when you commit to a pet you commit to them all the way, for their whole life."

Nodding, Marcie didn't look happy about the answer, but she wasn't upset either. "That's what I thought you'd say. That's pretty much what all my family and friends have been telling me too. I am going to see another doctor, but I have a feeling that I'll get the same answers. It's just kind of sad. He's a great guy and I could see us having a future together. You know...if not for the cats."

"Do you like cats?" asked one of the other attendees. "I mean, even if you didn't have allergies would you want to live with three cats?"

Marcie shrugged. "I have no idea if I like them or not. I've never been with one long enough to get an opinion."

The conversation veered again to discussing whether dog people should or should not be with cat people and vice versa. Out of the corner of her eye, she could see Luke's lips twitch. He found it amusing.

A pretty brunette sitting halfway down the table piped up. "I have a question. Who's the guy sitting in the corner?"

A ripple of laughter ran around the room and the brunette's

cheeks turned pink. Several of the others were nodding as if they had wanted to ask the question as well. Luke was sitting in his chair with a grin, his brows raised in question. They'd discussed this earlier, as Shaw had a feeling that someone might ask about his role since he wasn't participating, but ultimately he'd left it up to her to decide what she'd say. If anything.

Honesty was *usually* the best policy. To a certain extent.

"Luke is a good friend of mine and he's here to help me out today."

"Is he a psychologist too?" the brunette asked.

"No, he's a former law enforcement officer." She took a deep breath and plunged forward. "He's here to make sure that this meet and greet stays friendly and professional."

There were a few frowns and then the meaning of her words seemed to become clearer.

"You mean if a troll came here and harassed you?" Marcie queried. "I've seen some of those people in the comments section on your videos. They hate everything and everyone."

"Does that happen a lot?" another woman asked. "That must be awful."

"It's certainly not the best part of having a channel but it comes with the territory," Shaw explained. "I try to ignore the negative and concentrate on the positive."

Marcie's gaze wandered back to Luke. "Have you ever had to kick anyone out?"

"No, and I'm very grateful for that."

The brunette's attention was all on Luke. "You used to be a

cop? That's really cool. Do you have any interesting stories you can tell us?"

This was new…everyone was now paying attention to Luke. Which was fine, but they hadn't quite prepared for this line of questioning.

He shifted in his chair and rubbed at his chin. "I don't want to derail the discussion—"

"I have some questions too," Marcie said. "You hear all the time about how women need to be careful and that we shouldn't be out alone at night. My mother always told me to carry my keys in my hand, but would that really work if I was attacked?"

Actually, this was a good discussion. The room was mostly female except for a few men and her channel was all about helping people. People being safe was good.

"Luke, if you're comfortable answering these questions it's fine. I think this is excellent information and being safety conscious is important."

Stretching out his long legs, he sat up straight in the chair, his gaze intent. Clearly, he took this seriously.

"Okay, then I'll start with the first question. Yes, I have stories, and no, I won't tell you about them." A collective groan went up and Luke chuckled. "The reason I won't is that some of those cases are still pending. It's best to keep my mouth shut about them. Maybe I'll write a book when I retire in forty years or so. Now to get to the second question as to whether keys would help in an attack. That would depend on how you use them. If you try to stab them in the gut or the hand or the leg?

Nope. They're not going to care. Now if you use them to gouge his eyes out that just might work."

A few women wrinkled their noses at the image that his words probably created.

"I can see that you don't much like that," he said with a short laugh. "The thing is if you're being attacked, you're going to have to forget all the ladylike crap that's been shoved into your head your whole life and fight like you've never fought before. And when I say fight, I'm saying that you need to play down and dirty because he will, that's for sure. He won't care about rules or being squeamish. Knee him in the balls, use fingernails to scratch at his eyes, use the palm of your hand to break his nose. Yes, there will be blood but if that's what you need to get away then do it. Because the number one rule in being attacked is to never, under any circumstances, let them take you away from where you are."

He leaned forward, his elbows resting on his knees and his expression sober and serious.

"Attackers might want to take you away somewhere more secluded and quiet where they can take their time. You don't want that. Let me repeat those words because they're important as hell. You don't want that because that's how you die. You want to scream and fight and kick and yell. You want to be their worst nightmare of a target and make their lives hell. *You want to not be worth the hassle.* You want them to give up and run away."

"Wouldn't the best advice be to not be alone at night in the first place?" the brunette asked. "Then you don't have to worry about it."

"I guess if you only want to go out during the day, that's one way to do it, but not all attacks take place at night. Or with strangers. Just remember to listen to your intuition. If that little voice in the back of your head is telling you that something isn't quite right, listen to it. Whether you're on a date or having a drink or just sitting in a cafe having lunch. If something doesn't feel right, get out of there. Trust yourself. You're right more than you're wrong."

The discussion was lively and there were more questions, but eventually the conversation swung back to Shaw and abusive relationships. They talked about the signs of narcissism in a person and then it was time to end the meet and greet. She took a few more selfies and stood by the door to thank everyone for coming. Luke, as usual, stepped back and left her to it until they were the only two left.

"That wasn't too bad," Shaw said with a sigh of relief. Since she worked from home alone most of the time, she was exhausted at having to be "on" for that long. "They were all really nice. I don't think any one of them are my stalker."

"I agree." He held up his phone. "Ryan has been texting me every now and then and he hasn't seen anything out there either. No one loitering around looking aimless or acting strange. If he's out there, he's blending in perfectly."

"So this was a giant dead end?"

"As far as the case goes, but your fans adore you."

She felt the warmth in her cheeks. "I adore them too. If it

weren't for them, I wouldn't be able to do this. I feel so lucky."

"How about later I buy this lucky woman some dinner and we can play a game? I'll let you pick which one."

"You know I'm going to pick Trivial Pursuit."

"Then you're going to be the winner. Probably. You never know. My luck could turn on a dime."

That wouldn't be so bad. It could happen. Perhaps Shaw's stalker would suddenly reveal his identity and then she could get rid of him. Once and for all.

Until then, she had Luke to keep her safe.

★ ★ ★

THEIR PLANS, HOWEVER, were derailed when Luke received a call from the office. He needed to go as one of their cases was in *all hands on deck* mode. Nothing dangerous, he assured her, just intensive research that had to be done immediately. Since he didn't want her to be alone, he'd called Melissa and asked her to hang out. He'd even offered to buy the pizza. Both dogs' ears had perked up at one of their most favorite words.

Pizza.

"I love pizza," Melissa hummed as she took another cheesy bite. It all smelled amazing. What was not to like? Garlic, tomatoes, cheese. All good. "It's even better when my brother pays for it."

Shaw and Melissa were curled up on the couch, the pizza box open on the coffee table. Dylan and Murphy were right next to them hoping for a stray piece of sausage or a bite of cheese.

They'd get a more appropriate doggie snack later.

"He felt badly about leaving me alone tonight. I would have been fine with the dogs, but I'm glad you came over."

Melissa ruffled the fur behind Dylan's ear. "No one would get near this place with these two around, but I'm glad that we can hang out. I've been dying to ask how it's going with my big brother. Are there wedding bells yet? Should I start saving for a bridesmaid dress? You'll name the first one after me, right?"

Shaw could feel the telltale heat in her cheeks. She wasn't fooling anyone, least of all Melissa.

"It's going great. He's a wonderful man. So thank you for introducing us."

Giggling, Melissa shook her head. "I wasn't looking for a thank you. Just seeing you two together and so happy is good enough for me. You deserve it and my brother deserves it. You've both been alone too long."

"What about you? Don't you deserve to be happy?"

"I most certainly do," Melissa replied with mock indignation. "As a matter of fact, I've met a nice guy online. We're supposed to meet for coffee over the weekend. You never know. He could be the one."

The one thing about Melissa that Shaw loved was her friend's unbridled optimism. She had a lovely sunny personality that always thought the best of people and situations.

I should be more like her.

She'd been loath to bring it up with Melissa before but now that Shaw and Luke were getting closer it brought up more questions.

"Has Luke ever been really serious with a woman? Marriage serious?"

"Not really, although you could say he was serious about his high school girlfriend Celia. I'm sure they talked about the future more than once, but I don't think he was anywhere in the ballpark to propose. Since then he's dated but honestly, I've never been all the fond of his girlfriends. It's okay though because he hates all of the guys I date too."

"I hope you don't come to hate me."

"You? You're one of my favorite people."

Shaw reached for another slice of pizza. "What about Ryan? Is he one of your favorite people too?"

Rolling her eyes, Melissa laughed. "I like Ryan just fine, but it's not going to happen for us. I get more of a brotherly vibe with him. Not that he isn't handsome and sexy, because he totally is. He's just…I don't know. He doesn't do it for me for some reason. Frankly, no one is more puzzled by my reaction to him than I am. But there's zero chemistry there."

"I think Luke was hoping you two might hit it off."

"I think so too. Then he could finally like someone I'm dating but that's not going to happen. He's going to have to eventually deal with the guy when the time comes. I've already told him in no uncertain terms that his opinion doesn't matter."

Shaw didn't believe that for a second.

"At all?"

"Well, maybe a little but don't tell him that. Of course, I

want my family to like the man that I eventually marry but if they hate him and I love him then we'll just be Romeo and Juliet."

"They ended up dead at the end of that play. Along with about four other people."

"Like Romeo and Juliet. But not that part."

Those were words to live by. Shaw was determined that she and Luke were going to stay alive as well. All she needed was for her stalker to make one tiny mistake.

Was that too much to ask?

CHAPTER TWENTY-THREE

THE NEXT MORNING, Luke had dropped Shaw back at home so she could work. Once again he hadn't wanted to leave her, but she'd insisted she'd be fine. He'd tried to talk her into working out of his house but she simply had way too much equipment – lights, backdrop, and camera – to be able to do that. He'd personally walked around the house making sure all the windows and doors were locked before she was able to convince him to go to work.

Shaw was busy editing the new video when she received a call from Oliver. She braced herself for whatever he was going to say, doubtful it was anything positive. He'd only called her a handful of times all these months and it had never been good news. Usually he was passing on a message about how disappointed Julia was regarding Shaw's behavior and if she could just apologize that would be great.

I am not apologizing this time.

"Hi, Oliver. What can I do for you?"

"Thank goodness you're home." There was relief in his tone as if he'd been pacing the floor worrying about her whereabouts.

"Your poor mother has been sick all morning. A little feverish and some body aches. Stuffy nose too. I hate to ask you this, but I don't suppose you could run and get that chicken soup Julia loves so much and bring it over? I'd go myself but I hate to leave her when she's not feeling well."

A sick Julia was far worse than a healthy Julia. Poor Oliver.

"Does she need to go to the hospital? How high is her fever?"

"Not that high," her stepfather assured Shaw. "I've been monitoring it. She's just feeling miserable and says that her throat hurts so the steaks we were going to have for dinner are definitely out. I know that you're busy and all, and I hate to ask, but I'm kind of desperate here."

Of all people Shaw understood. Oliver seemed like a nice man, but no one could be prepared for the first time Julia was sick. The second time he would know what to expect.

"It's fine. I'll do it," Shaw replied, already standing to grab a coat and scarf. Where were her keys? Right...on the kitchen counter. "Can I pick up anything else? Cold medicine? Tissues?"

"We're good on all of that. I'm just forever grateful that you'll bring the soup. It's going to mean so much to your mother that you're coming by too. I'll go let her know. Drive carefully."

What Oliver didn't know – and Shaw wasn't going to tell him – was that the soup would only give temporary relief. Once it was gone, Julia was going to demand fluffed pillows, different blankets, and perfectly brewed tea.

"I will. See you soon."

She grabbed her purse and headed to her car, pausing to

briefly send off a quick text to Luke, letting him know that she was running to her mother's house.

Mom is sick.
Poor Oliver.
I'm taking soup.
Then I'll be back.
Order in dinner?

His reply was a thumbs up so all was good. She hadn't wanted to disturb him at work, but she didn't use her phone when she was driving. With everything going on, she didn't want him to worry if he sent a text and she didn't reply right away.

Stopping on the way to pick up a to-go order of the chicken soup, it took about forty-five minutes to reach her mother's home. Located on a ten-acre lot, far away from the rush of Seattle but close enough to go into the city for the day without having to spend the night, the house was a mid-century modern design with lots of wood and glass. The lot was mostly trees which were bare this time of year but there were a few outbuildings that had been on the property when Julia and Oliver had bought the place about nine months ago. They'd been enthusiastic when they'd moved in, but the shine had quickly worn away and they'd found a dozen little things that bothered them.

One of those items was the long winding driveway from the road to the house. In the autumn, Shaw found it breathtaking with the colored leaves creating a canopy over the narrow path, but she had to admit in the winter it looked far more forbidding, almost creepy with the gray skies overhead.

After parking in front of the house, she climbed the steps and rang the doorbell. There was no answer so she pushed open the door a crack and called out to Oliver. He was probably upstairs with her mother.

"Come on in," he yelled from deeper in the home. "I'm in the kitchen making your mother some tea. Do you want one too?"

"I'm good," she called back, shrugging off her coat. "I've got the soup."

Oliver was pouring hot water into a large mug. "Your mother is going to be happy to see that soup and to see you. You made good time. Not much traffic?"

"It wasn't too bad. Where is Mom?"

"She's upstairs asleep. Why don't you sit for a little while? She'll be awake soon."

Shaw held up the styrofoam container. "Should I put this in the refrigerator then?"

"She won't be asleep long. Just leave it there. Sit and relax. She'll wake up soon."

It started as a tingle on the back of Shaw's neck. Nothing major, just a small feeling of unease. Oliver wasn't making eye contact with her which was unusual. Even his tone of voice was slightly off, as if he was forcing himself to sound cheerful and nonchalant.

"Mom's okay, right? It's just a cold?"

Could he be hiding how ill her mother was? Normally Julia

was quite vocal when she was sick.

"Why would you think otherwise? She's fine. It's only a common cold. She'll feel better in a few days." He pulled open the door of the refrigerator. "I'll pour you some iced tea."

Shaw really didn't want tea. She wanted answers.

"Is everything okay, Oliver? You seem tense."

He poured tea into a tumbler. "I'm fine. Why do you ask?"

He kept answering questions with questions, sending them round in a circle.

"Because you seem tense," she repeated. "Not quite your-self."

There was that tingle again, this time far more insistent. She remembered back to Luke at the meet and greet where he'd talked about intuition and how people often didn't listen to theirs. Her ears were wide open at the moment. She wasn't going to ignore it.

"Is Mom really okay?"

The fact that Julia wasn't anywhere to be seen was strange. She normally wouldn't take a nap if she knew Shaw was coming over.

To her shock, Oliver slammed down the iced tea glass on the kitchen counter, the liquid sloshing over the side and onto the granite.

"I fucking said she's okay," he yelled. "Stop asking me questions about your mother."

Holy shit. She'd never seen Oliver even remotely upset, and now he was mad. His face was red and his lips were pulled back in a snarl, baring his teeth. Shaw's heart accelerated and her stomach twisted into a knot. And that tingle? It was an all-out pain in the back of her neck now, screaming at her to get the hell out of that house and go home. She didn't like her stepfather when he was in this mood.

"Okay," she replied in her most soothing tone. "You know me, I'm just worried about Mom. It's all good. So...yeah...I think I'll head home and call her later when she's up from her nap. Obviously, if she's sick she needs her rest."

"You can't go."

"I'll call Mom later," she assured him, taking a small step back. She didn't want to upset him even more with any sudden movements. He still appeared to be furious with her. "And I'll get out of your hair. I'm sure you're really busy."

By the time she'd realized his hand had snaked out and grabbed her by the arm it was too late. His grip was too tight to be shaken off easily, although she'd tried to yank it back.

Sweat pooled at the back of her neck and her heart thudded in her ears. She had a bad feeling about this. Very bad. This wasn't right. Looking into his eyes, they appeared cold and glassy. Almost dead.

"You can't go," he repeated, his grip punishing as she twisted her arm to loosen his hold. "I'm tired of you ignoring me, acting like you're better than everyone. You don't get to treat me this way. You need to understand."

She was beginning to understand a whole bunch and none of it was good.

I'm ignoring you?

"I want to understand. Why don't you help me?"

Dammit, Shaw had left her car keys on the foyer table along with her coat. Also, the kitchen was at the rear of the house so she would have to run back through to get to her keys and out the front door to get to her car. Just how far was it? How long would it take her? She was in good shape and much younger than Oliver but if he caught up to her before she could get away?

He jerked her arm again, twisting it painfully. She was going to be a mass of bruises tomorrow.

If I live that long.

"Don't patronize me. I've reached out to you over and over again, but you've always ignored me. I've made you my whole life. Ignored my messages and gifts."

Shit, was he…?

"I didn't mean to ignore you, Oliver. And I want to help you. Tell me how I can help you."

Her voice sounded high, breathless, and squeaky. It shook far too much and he had to know that he was scaring her. It looked like that was the plan.

"You gave your attention to him," he said, his face so close to hers she could feel his coffee-soaked breath. His tone was accusing as if she'd mortally wounded him. "Him. He was all you could think about, wasn't he? I saw the way that you looked at him. You ignored me, Shaw. I'd do anything for you. He wouldn't do what I've done. He couldn't even understand what I've sacrificed for you. I knew the minute your mother showed me one of your videos that we were meant to be. It was fate that brought us together. Can't you see that? Can't you see it?"

Oliver was shouting now, his face a mask of anger and frustration. A wash of cold fear ran through Shaw's veins, her brain frantically working on a way out of this situation. Luke wasn't here to save her and heaven only knew where her mother was. Or what Oliver might have done with her…

Her stepfather was her stalker.

And she'd walked right into his home. Right into the lion's den.

Make than an unstable lion. He was clearly deluded.

"I can see it," she said, keeping her voice down and calm. It wasn't easy. She wanted to scream and yell. She wanted to run but she doubted she'd get far. She was going to have to use her brain to get out of this. "I can totally see it now. I just didn't realize it before. But I can see it now. I didn't mean to ignore you. I'm really sorry about that. I won't ignore you anymore."

His expression scrunched up, his eyes narrowing. "You think I'm stupid, but I'm not. I know that you only want him. You're just playing with me. I'm not going to let you make a fool of me, Shaw."

Shit, she had to do something. Right now. He wasn't buying her bullshit.

Her brain cranked through several scenarios, but she discarded each one as flawed. He wasn't going to let go of her easily and even if he did, he probably wasn't going to let her walk out of there. At this point, his behavior was completely unpredictable.

She had no idea what he'd do next.

That's what made him so dangerous. That's why she needed to get out of here. Sooner rather than later. Every instinct that she possessed was standing up and yelling at her to get out of there, run, hide, do whatever she had to do, but do not stay. She could feel the hairs stand up on her arm one after the other, the gooseflesh rising as she contemplated her few options. None of them were any good.

The front door was too far but the back door… She might be able to make it if she could get him to let go. She needed just a second, a single distraction and then she could dart outside. There were lots of trees she might be able to hide behind and eventually, if she ran far enough, there would be neighbors. It was a long shot, but he was older and she was pretty sure he didn't work out or go to the gym.

But how to distract him? She couldn't just point to the window and say, "Hey, what's that?" That only worked in the movies. Her gaze frantically ran around the kitchen and then rested on the styrofoam container of hot soup sitting right next to her on the kitchen counter. It wouldn't be burning hot but it would be warm enough.

I just need a head start.

Inching her right hand closer to the container, she moved her head so that she was looking directly into Oliver's eyes. Hopefully blocking his view of her arm. She could hear the roar of her heartbeat inside her head, feel the blood whipping through her veins. Every sense she had was fine tuned to this moment and place. She had to choose the exact right second.

"I don't think you're stupid at all. Obviously, you're an intelligent and successful man. I just don't know you as well as I should. We should talk and get to know each other better. Is my mom out for the afternoon? Will we be interrupted? Or is she here in the house?"

Hopefully alive and well. Hopefully she just went shopping or to run an errand. Please let her be okay.

"We won't be interrupted. We—"

He didn't get any further. Adrenaline pumping, Shaw's trembling fingers curled around the container. She'd only get one shot at this. As quietly as possible, her thumb flicked off the lid just enough. She sucked in a breath and hurled the soup with all of her might directly into his face, aiming right for his eyes.

Don't take the time to celebrate.

Howling with pain and fury, Oliver dropped her arm and raised his hands to his face to wipe away the chicken soup that was currently dripping down his chin and onto the floor. She didn't wait around to see how successful he was going to be. Darting far enough away that he couldn't reach her with an outstretched limb, she ran to the back door and didn't look back. The nearest neighbor was to the right and that's where she headed.

The frigid outdoor air hit any exposed flesh immediately, almost sending her to her knees. Stumbling for a moment on a tree root, she righted herself and took a quick look over her shoulder. He was exiting the house.

The chase was on, and this was one race she couldn't afford to lose.

CHAPTER TWENTY-FOUR

INVESTIGATIVE WORK COULD be tedious as hell. Long hours, lots of coffee, and even more research. If Luke was working a cold case, he might be elbow deep in dusty old files that had been stuck in boxes in some dark warehouse somewhere. Today, however, he was hunched over his laptop running license plate numbers from the red light cameras outside of the sports bar, and damn, if that wasn't a busy as hell street.

He'd already run the lights to the west and the north and was now about halfway through the east. So far, he hadn't found anything much. There were a handful of names that had police records, and he'd set them aside to look at more in-depth, but frankly he'd been hoping to see Eric Bishop or James Hornsby. At this point, Luke would have been happy to find anyone even remotely connected to Shaw whether her barista, mail carrier, or pizza delivery guy.

So far, Luke had hit one wall after another trying to figure out who was harassing and stalking Shaw. It didn't say much for his investigative skills that he couldn't find one lone male that was pissing him off royally. Logan and Reed were probably trying to figure out a way to get rid of him but in a nice way.

Shaw was being patient as well, but he could see that the stress was taking its toll on her. She wasn't as quick to smile and the shadows under her eyes seemed darker and more pronounced.

And Luke? He wanted this whole clusterfuck to be over once and for all. He hated to see Shaw this upset and scared. She didn't deserve this. She was too wonderful to have all of this shit happening to her.

He was falling for her. Hard and fast. It hadn't been long, but Luke wasn't a kid anymore. He knew what he was looking for in a woman and what he didn't want. This wasn't about the sex – although that was off the charts good. It wasn't about whether she was beautiful or anything like that.

It was how he felt when they were together. It was as if she was the puzzle piece that had been missing from his life. She was all the things he hadn't even known he wanted but now that she was here, he didn't want to be without her for a single day.

Yeah, I have it bad. But I don't care.

It wasn't the greatest time in his life to fall in love and have a committed relationship, but it wasn't the worst either. They could make it work if they wanted to…and he definitely wanted to. Did Shaw? All signs pointed to his feelings being returned, but until her life was stalker-free their relationship had to wait on the back burner. It wouldn't be fair to ask for more right now.

Heaving a sigh, he checked the computer program running the plate numbers and spitting out names one after the other.

Eighty-six percent done. It would be finished in a few minutes. Maybe he'd order in a sandwich so he could go through the names with records. He'd missed lunch. Again.

"I'm glad you're here. I found something."

With a grin on his face Ryan bounded into the room, holding up a photo.

"I could use some good news. What do you have?"

Plopping down in the chair next to Luke, Ryan held out the picture. "I was looking at all of the footage from the last few days around Shaw's house. Guess what I found? Her friendly neighbor from across the street hanging around her back door and looking in her sliding glass windows."

Luke's heart leaped with excitement. This might be the break they were waiting on. Hornsby. He'd acted weird and now he was looking into Shaw's windows when she wasn't home?

"Let's give this to the police. They can bring him in and question him," Luke said, studying the photo of Hornsby with his nose pressed up to Shaw's windows. Ick. "I'd love to do it myself, but I think we might just piss them off and we need to keep a good relationship with them."

Ryan grimaced. "Can I say that it's incredibly creepy that he's peeping in her windows? Christ, that's perverted."

"I knew there was something wrong with that guy." Luke reached for the phone. "I'll call the investigator in charge—"

His hand hovered over his phone, the name that popped up on the laptop screen capturing his attention.

"Are you okay?"

Luke's arm dropped to his side. "I don't think so. Look at the name that the computer found. I was looking through the plates that went through the red light cameras around the bar."

Leaning down, Ryan squinted to read the name. "Oliver Stephenson. You've lost me. Who is he? Another ex-boyfriend?"

"No, he's her stepfather."

"They live in the area, right? It might just be a—"

"Coincidence," Luke finished for him. "You know what Logan says about coincidences. And no, they don't live in that area."

His gut agreed. The older affable man didn't fit the usual image of a stalker but what did they really know about him? Not much.

"I don't like coincidences that much either," Ryan said, shaking his head. "What are you going to do now?"

That feeling of foreboding had come over Luke. He didn't like this, and he sure as shit didn't want Shaw anywhere near Oliver Stephenson until they checked him out thoroughly.

"Shaw sent me a text a little while ago. She was going to get some soup and take it to her mother. Oliver asked her to." Decision made. "I'm heading there right now. I don't want him in the same room as she is until we've cleared him."

Ryan held up the photo. "What about Hornsby? He's a peeper at the very least."

He was but he wasn't an immediate threat to Shaw. Stephenson was.

"We'll deal with him later. Right now, I want to get to

Shaw."

"Then I'm going with you."

"I hope I won't need your help."

"I hope you don't either."

But just in case, it wouldn't hurt. In mere minutes they now had two suspects. Only one could be the stalker. Was it the creepy neighbor or the easygoing stepfather?

Time to find out.

SHAW HAD A painful stitch in her side and her lungs ached so badly she could barely suck in oxygen. She'd never been much of a runner, but no one had warned her that running in the cold winter air was far different than a jog on a spring day.

It just plain hurt.

When she'd pictured hiding behind trees, her brain hadn't quite put together the fact that there weren't any leaves on those trees. The bushes and shrubbery were bare. There wasn't much to hide behind so she'd had to keep running, only taking a break here and there to hide behind a big rock or a big tree trunk.

The entire time she could hear the thud of his feet on the damp ground, persistent and relentless. It was only when he stopped to take a breath that she felt safe enough to do the same. She couldn't see him from where she was at the moment but she could hear him, the footsteps sounding like drums in her ears.

If I don't catch my breath soon I'm going to puke.

He paused again and this time she ducked behind a gathering of rocks, trying to catch her breath. She couldn't keep this up indefinitely. With the way he'd been chasing her, she'd had to move side to side which meant she wasn't nearly as close to the neighbor's house as she'd hoped to be by now. She might need another plan. A better one.

Luke's words were now haunting her, coming back loudly and clearly in her head.

Don't let them take you anywhere. Fight for your life if you have to. Play dirty because he will too. Hit them in the most vulnerable areas. Scream, yell, and don't go quietly. Make it as hard as it could possibly be.

Quickly scanning the area, Shaw realized that she was closer to the road than the neighbor's house. It might be better to head there, out in the open instead of back here among all of these trees. Would Oliver try to hurt her in broad daylight on an open road?

She had no idea the answer to that but if she went to the neighbor's home and no one was there, she'd be shit out of luck. She'd then have to make another run for the road to get to other people.

So I'm going to run to the road.

Decision made. Whether it was a good one or not was still to be seen. She could hear Oliver's footsteps again, slower this time though. He had to be as fatigued as she was, if not more. She needed to slow him down a little, but she didn't have any more soup.

A branch. One was lying on the ground within reach. It

wasn't so big that she couldn't lift it, but it was large enough that it might do some damage if she gave it a major league swing or two.

Fight for your life if you have to.

She didn't know what Oliver had planned for her, but all indications were that it wasn't anything good. Heaven only knew what he'd done to her mother. She might be out shopping or she might be hurt somewhere. To find out, Shaw had to find someone to help them.

Turning so she could peek over the top of the rocks, she reached for the branch, dragging it closer to her and wrapping both hands tightly around the rough bark. Oliver had paused for a second, puffs of fog coming from his mouth as he breathed heavily. He looked right and then left, then right again, spying the rocks. She ducked back down but it wouldn't make any difference. He was going to run straight for her location. It was the only logical place for her to be.

Time to fight.

Closing her eyes for a brief moment, she gathered all of her courage and energy. There would be no dress rehearsal. This was it. Failing wasn't an option.

She took a cleansing breath and adjusted her grip just as he rounded the rock formation. Leaping to her feet, she twisted her body and pulled the branch back before throwing all her weight forward, the thick wood whistling through the air and crashing right into Oliver's knees. He went down with a scream of pain, immediately curling into a fetal position to protect himself, cursing her the entire time. Another blow wouldn't do much more damage and she had the head start she'd been needing.

"You fucking bitch!"

Tossing the branch away from his reach, she took off for the road as fast as she possibly could. She'd had a short rest and she needed to push her body far past what she'd ever thought she could do.

Pumping her arms and breathing fast, she raced through the bare trees, her gaze on the ground so she wouldn't trip over a random tree root, rock, or branch. Just a few feet away she could see the end of the grass and the beginning of pavement. She was so close.

Blood roared in her ears but the rest of her body had gone numb with cold. Every single step was like shoving knives in her feet and legs but she couldn't give in, she couldn't stop. Was Oliver behind her? Was he still lying on the ground? She couldn't hear his footsteps behind her but then she couldn't hear anything but the sound of her own heartbeat as loud as a marching band in a parade.

The first step onto the pavement was a relief but she wasn't home free yet. She turned to her left, so she was running towards traffic and almost screamed with relief when she saw a vehicle in the distance. Placing herself in the middle of the lane, she ran to it, waving her arms and jumping up and down.

The car braked and swerved but halted, two familiar men jumping out of it. Luke and Ryan. She didn't know how they were there but she was so happy to see them.

With no more energy to be had, she fell onto her knees in the road, her entire body shaking in delayed reaction. She hadn't even realized she was crying until she touched her face but her cheeks were all wet.

"Baby, I'm here." Luke had scooped her up in his arms and was cradling her to his chest. "I'm here. No one is going to hurt you now. No one."

"Oliver," she said, but the words weren't coming out very well. Her voice was a mere croak because of all of the cold air and she was still trembling, her hands not able to grip his shirt. She wanted to touch him to make sure he was real. For a moment, she thought that perhaps her imagination had conjured him up in desperation but the warmth from his body was beginning to seep through her clothes and she was beginning to believe that this might be real.

"Where is he, Shaw?" Ryan asked, his gaze darting around the area. "Point me in the right direction."

It took tremendous effort to raise her arm. "My mother. I don't know where she is."

Ryan nodded and took off into the trees where she'd just exited. Luke strode back to the vehicle and tucked her into the passenger side before climbing into the driver's seat.

"I'm taking you back to the house." He picked up his cell and thumbed the screen. "I'm also going to call the police. We'll find your mom, Shaw. Don't worry."

Worry? She didn't even know where to begin worrying.

"I feel numb."

He gave her a reassuring smile. "That's probably a good thing, honey. It will hit you later but we'll deal with it then. Just know that I'm here for you, okay?"

Luke was here. He wasn't a figment of her imagination. Unfortunately, none of this was make believe. The entire scenario was almost too far-fetched to be real, but it was. She'd lived it.

She was alive. She'd survived. But now what?

Shaw didn't know what she was supposed to do next.

CHAPTER TWENTY-FIVE

THE COLOR WAS beginning to come back into Shaw's cheeks. Luke had been worried about her for the last few hours. She'd barely spoken except to tell her story to him and Ryan, and then the police. He didn't want to push her though. She'd been through enough without him being a jerk.

When he'd seen her running toward them on that road, flailing her arms in the air… Shit, he couldn't even begin to describe the fear and panic he'd felt. Fear that she'd been hurt and panic that he wouldn't be able to help her, protect her. There was anger too – at himself and at Stephenson.

I should have known. Somehow. I should have.

He was supposed to be an expert, a professional but he hadn't seen anything sinister in Oliver Stephenson. Perhaps that was how the older man was so effective; he'd been hiding in plain sight.

One thing he was sure of though was that this woman was the most important thing in his life. He hadn't known her long, but he knew for sure that he wanted a future with her. He could only hope that she felt the same.

When they'd arrived back at the house, he'd helped Shaw inside and wrapped her in a blanket that had hung off the back of a chair before searching through every room for her mother. Luckily, he'd found Julia sleeping in the master bedroom, but he couldn't rouse her. Suspecting that she'd been drugged by her husband, he called an ambulance. She was breathing fine and didn't appear injured in any way, but she definitely needed to see a medical professional.

He'd gone back downstairs and assured Shaw that her mother was alive. That numbness that she'd talked about earlier had to still be in residence because she simply nodded and thanked him. It was then that Ryan showed up, dragging a limping but angry Oliver with him. The older man had been cuffed and they sat him down on the back porch while he raved and ranted against the world in general and Shaw in particular.

Luke let Ryan deal with Oliver and he stayed close to Shaw until the police and the ambulance arrived. There were statements to make of course, questions that needed answering. Julia was loaded into an ambulance and by that time she'd woken up confused and disoriented, but quite alive.

She couldn't answer any questions as to what happened to her but Shaw was able to describe how she'd been lured to the house by Oliver, telling her that her mother was ill and wanted soup. She told them how she'd realized that he was the stalker and also how she'd thrown soup in his face to run out of the house. Then she'd smacked his knees with a tree branch. He was almost bursting with pride when she described her escape. She'd done what needed to be done.

Now she needed him to take care of her. All the adrenaline had to have drained from her body by now and that numbness would eventually leave too. She was going to need him and her friends to help her through this traumatic event.

I wouldn't be anywhere else.

"Do you want some more tea?" he asked, gently tucking the blanket around her knees. He'd brought her back to his place and stationed her on the couch. The dogs had immediately picked up on her distress and they'd taken up residence on either side of her as if to protect her from the outside world. "I could make you some toast."

She shook her head and placed the empty cup on the end table. "No, I'm fine."

She wasn't fine. At all.

"Honey, it's okay to be upset."

"I know that." She pointed to her temple. "In my head, I know that, but there's a little voice in there too that's been telling me that I need to hold it all together. That I can't let myself cry or break down. Even though I cried before."

"That little voice sounds like a real pain in the ass."

It was a joke and she gave him a small smile in return.

"It is," she agreed. "I can't help but feel..." He didn't prompt her or interrupt, letting her piece her thoughts together in her own time. "I can't help but feel like this is all my own fault."

He sat down next to her, moving Murphy to do so. "This is

no one's fault by your stepfather's. No one, Shaw. He's to blame here."

"My mother–"

"Is going to be fine. They're keeping her overnight for observation. That's all. She'll be out tomorrow."

"But I'm the reason–"

"No," he said firmly. "You are not the reason she's in the hospital. Shit, she brought him into your life, not the other way around. The blame is his. You and your mother are victims."

She wrinkled her nose. "I don't much like being a victim, to tell you the truth."

"Then don't be one. But don't discount what you've experienced here today. That's something that you're going to have to grapple with. What would you tell someone that wrote in to you for advice if they were in this situation?"

"I'd tell them to see a therapist."

"Sounds like a good idea to me. It couldn't hurt."

She sat back against the cushions. "What happens now, Luke?"

A good question. Luke had been thinking about that himself.

"Your stepfather has been arrested. He'll probably make bail, to be honest. If you and your mother press charges, there might be a trial but more likely he'll make a deal. He'll promise to stay away from both of you in exchange for probation and community service."

Shaw's mouth fell open. "Community service? Probation? He won't go to jail?"

Luke had to be honest. "If it's his first offense? Probably not. I won't lie to you about that. Now if he has a history of doing this, then it might be different. My bet is he's done this before."

"He probably has," she agreed. "But if he's never been in trouble for it before…"

Her voice trailed off with a soft sigh. She was right. This wasn't fair.

"I'm going to dig into his background, sweetheart. If he's done this before, we'll find it and give it to the district attorney. I'll do what I can to make this stick."

"What if he doesn't leave me alone?"

"Then I'll kill him," Luke growled, his teeth snapped together in a snarl. "I'll make him wish that he was a thousand miles away. Now that we know who was stalking you, he's never going to get near you again. I promise you that, Shaw."

"I'm going to hold you to that." She reached out for his hand, their fingers tangling. "Have I thanked you yet for coming to my rescue?"

Snuggling closer, he pressed a kiss to the satin skin of her forehead. "No thanks needed. I was glad I was there. But I have to be honest, I don't think you needed my help. You handled Stephenson just fine. You put a major hurt on him. You could be the star in an action flick."

Giggling, she placed her cheek on his shoulder and his heart almost burst from his chest. The feelings that he had for this woman were so incredibly strong. She was the one. He knew it deep inside.

"I don't think so, but I tried to take your advice."

"You did great, honey. I'm really proud of you."

"I'm proud of me too." Shaw yawned widely and then laughed. "I don't know why I'm yawning. I'm not tired. I mean, I am exhausted but there's no way that I could go to sleep now."

"I could order a pizza," Luke suggested. "We could play Monopoly if you want. I might even let you win."

Murphy and Dylan both jumped to attention at one of their favorite words. *Pizza.* The canines' tails were wagging furiously. Their expression could only be described as hopeful.

"Maybe later." She wrapped her arm around him, cuddling even closer. "I just want to lie here in your arms for awhile. When I first saw you on that road today I thought I had conjured you out of my imagination. But you're really here."

Luke was here, and he wasn't going anywhere. This woman had stolen his heart and he didn't want it back.

He'd hold her for as long as she'd let him.

IT WAS VEGAS, baby.

Two months ago Shaw would have never thought she would be sitting in a fancy steakhouse inside of an even fancier hotel in Las Vegas but then her life had taken quite a few twists and turns in that time. Some of them for the better, and a few... Well, time would tell the tale.

"To us and to Vegas," Luke said, lifting his glass of beer. "And to steaks, medium rare."

"I'll drink to that," she giggled, lifting her own pomegranate martini to clink glasses. "But only if we can get baked potatoes too."

"Of course. You can't have one without the other."

Leaning down, Luke brushed Shaw's lips with his own. As always, she was swamped by emotions whenever he was near. He'd been a rock through all of this, never wavering in his support.

And love?

They hadn't said it yet, but she was sure they both felt it. If this was how he treated a woman he *wasn't* in love with then she'd love to see what he'd do when he'd fallen. She'd been planning for weeks to tell him on this trip how she felt. Despite being sure that her feelings were returned it was a little scary. Stepping out onto the edge of cliff scary. Once she said the words she couldn't take them back.

Oops! I was just kidding. Ignore what I said.

Their relationship had already moved forward a great deal, but this was going to send it into a whole other level. Love was the real deal. It meant a commitment for both of them. They would instantly become a serious couple. Not that they weren't serious now. After all, no man could have been more devoted than Luke had.

She'd been practicing how and when she would say it but so far, she hadn't found the right moment. Was this it?

"I'm so glad we were able to get away on this vacation," Luke said, settling back into his chair but keeping ahold of her hand, their fingers entwined. He looked so handsome this evening, dressed in a blue suit and an ivory silk tie. It wasn't his usual attire but the minute he'd put it on she'd been more than a bit heated. If he dressed like this all the time, they'd never make it out of the house. "We deserved it, don't you think?"

"We definitely did, although you more than me. You closed that cold case Logan and Reed gave you. I bet you're going to make the permanent team."

He'd explained that his assignment to the special task force was contingent on success and so far, from what she could see, he'd found it. He'd certainly wrapped up her issues in a timely manner.

"We'll see." Luke shrugged as if it didn't matter but she knew it did. He had a tremendous drive to succeed. "The other guys are damn good at their jobs too."

His phone buzzed and he checked it quickly, a grin crossing his handsome features before holding it up to show her.

A photo of Dylan and Murphy. Melissa was watching the two canines and they were each wearing signs that said how much they missed their daddy and Shaw.

"She's probably giving them cheese every day," Shaw warned him. "You know she spoils them."

"She does and they love it, but she says it's an aunt's prerogative. Family and all that."

Family. That was a subject that Shaw was beginning to believe she truly didn't understand. After Oliver had been arrested, she'd assumed that her mother would be outraged by what he'd done and leave him.

Not at all. Instead, Julia had defended him – even after spending a night in the hospital – and had blamed Shaw for everything that happened. She'd said that Shaw had somehow led Oliver on and her actions had brought this on herself.

In the ultimate action of boundary setting, Shaw had finally had no choice but to cut her mother out of her life. Julia wasn't going to change, or at least she wasn't going to change anytime in the near future. She could never take any blame herself and Shaw could never do anything right. It was a recipe for a poor relationship. Luckily, Shaw's friends had rallied around her and Luke and Melissa had offered up their own parents as surrogates.

As for Oliver, there had been talk of making a deal with the prosecutor, but Luke had found a treasure trove of information about her stepfather and none of it was good. First of all, his name wasn't Oliver Stephenson. Second, he had a history of harassing women in a few other states. Stealing their personal possessions – he'd admitted to stealing her blue scarf, among other things – and keeping them as some sort of creepy souvenirs. He'd also skipped out on court-mandated therapy over ten years ago. It was looking like this time he might actually go to jail. Julia was standing by him.

As for Shaw's neighbor James Hornsby, he'd sworn up and down that he was looking in her windows because he was worried about her, not that he was trying to be a pervert. Shaw had declined to press any charges. She'd wanted to put it all behind her. The police had given Hornsby a stern warning to stay away. If they hadn't, she was sure that Luke would have gladly done the job.

Whether her neighbor had been truly worried or was a big creep was a question they might never get the answer to. A few days later Hornsby had left on a long vacation and then a month ago a For Sale sign had gone up on his house. She wouldn't be sorry when he was gone.

As for her ex Eric Bishop she hadn't heard from him since, so he must have received the message that she wasn't interested. Taylor's boyfriend Austin turned out to be married with three kids. She'd dumped him immediately despite his begging and pleading that it was simply a misunderstanding. Melissa was seeing a guy she'd met at the gym and so far they seemed happy.

"We should pick them up a couple of t-shirts in the gift shop," Shaw suggested. "They'd look adorable."

"We'll have to get Melissa a matching one and put all three of them in a photo for my parents."

Luke's mom and dad adored their granddogs.

Fiddling with the stem of her martini glass, Shaw tried to gather her courage to tell Luke how she felt about him. This was a romantic meal in a fancy restaurant. This had to be a good time to take the leap.

"Are you okay, honey? You seem a little distant tonight."

This was her opening. Right here. Taking a fortifying drink of her martini, she placed the glass down and took a deep breath.

"Actually, there was something that I wanted to tell you."

"Don't say it."

What? Huh?

He rubbed the back of his neck, his smile sheepish. "I mean…shit…I think I know what you're going to say. Dammit, I should have said it a long time ago. I should have said it every day for the last two months. Shaw, I love you."

A thousand butterfly wings flew free in her abdomen and her heart fluttered in her chest.

"I love you too."

Luke was grinning ear to ear as if she'd given him a terrific Christmas present. "If we weren't sitting in a public restaurant, I'd grab you and take you straight to bed."

It was tempting. Luke and a comfortable mattress or this fancy, expensive meal. They hadn't ordered any food yet.

"I might be persuaded."

"Are you serious? Because I can throw down some cash for these drinks."

"Do it."

They could order a pizza later. Shaw would rather have fast food with this man than chateaubriand with anyone else.

She loved him that much.

I hope you enjoyed Lethal Allure. Don't miss the next book in the Serials and Stalkers series – Gilded Craving. Coming soon!

Thank you for reading.

Don't miss a thing! Sign up to be notified of Olivia's new releases:

Mailing List: oliviajaymes.com/News.html

ABOUT THE AUTHOR

Olivia Jaymes is a wife, mother, lover of sexy romance and cozy mysteries, and caffeine addict. She lives with her husband, son, and two spoiled dogs in central Florida and spends her days typing on her computer with a canine on her lap.

She is currently working on a new cozy mystery series – *A Ravenmist Whodunit* – in addition to her other ongoing romance series.

Visit Olivia Jaymes at

www.OliviaJaymes.com